TO BE

YOUNG,

PRIVILEGED,

& WOKE

ADRIENNE L. BILLINGS-SMITH

*"The revolution has always been
in the hands of the young.
The young always inherit the revolution."*

Huey Newton,
Co-Founder of the Black Panther Party.

Dedication

This book is dedicated to
Bubs and Boo Thang:

May you forever be young.
May you forever fight for what's right.
May you forever take care of one another.

My hope for you both
is a life full of love and success.

Acknowledgements

As I sat on my jumpseat in the dark and lay in my hotel rooms in Central America, Middle America, and beyond, I dug deep into my own experiences. I thought of the life I had, dreamt of, and have been trying to create for my own son and niece. I thought about all the kids out there who don't feel like they belong. I thought of my friends with the same experiences...not quite black enough and definitely not white enough. I thought about the culture that my grandfather, mother, aunt, and uncle raised me in. The beautiful life they had experienced through music and navigating their own Blackness.

Music is what held us together; music is what got me through days when I didn't want to go on; music is what helped me through heartbreak and love. I thought about the journey of all of those who came before me and all of those who will come behind me. I want to thank my wife for always being on this ride with me and letting me just be me. I thank my friends who continue to love me through it all. But most importantly I thank my Mom, who has always said "ok:" to whatever wild emotional ride I have taken her on. There is no me without you!

Contents

Chapter 1

Beyoncé

"We need to reshape our own perception of how we view ourselves. We have to step up as women and take the lead."

- Beyoncé Knowles.

"Ari! Get up! It's time for school, sweetie."

I could hear my mom's voice echo in a distant corner of my mind, brimming with warmth and comfort, but I was far too lost in an amazing, too-good-to-be-true dream. In the pleasant haze behind my closed eyelids, Beyonce was singing Halo to me like I was the only one in the crowd. The spotlight beamed at her, and she looked at me, cooing her beautiful song, and I kept singing my heart out, "Ariana Rena!" A less pleasant voice, my mom's, kept interrupting my dream. "Get your butt up now! You're going to be late for school!" My mom yells, a little less warm and comforting this time.

"Ughhh!" I grunt and roll over, trying to ignore the interruption, but I can't, so I finally open my eyelids, and just like that, I'm back to reality...I sit up on the side of the bed, my headscarf halfway off of my head.

What is the point of these things anyway?

I always wake up with them either "to the left, to the left..." ha it's going to be a good day, or the thing is lost somewhere in the bed. I stretch and slip into my warm house shoes and ask Alexa to play my Morning Beyoncé mix. My day always has to start with The Queen Bey. She literally gives me life. She has already written the soundtrack to my life sans Jay's cheating behind. As the music blares through the speakers, a smile starts to form on my lips. Hearing the familiar notes, I can already tell— it's going to be a good day. One day, I hope this string of good mornings leads me to my life's goal, which is to be Blue Ivy's personal stylist, so every day for me is Beyoncé Day without any distractions.

I pull the scarf off my head and exchange it for a shower cap. While in the shower, I think about what I'll wear to inspire my people today. This black girl magic doesn't come easily, you know. Unreliable headscarves, silk blowouts one week, Jill Scott' fros the next; one day, I think I'm just going to Sana'a Lathan this hair (chop-chop). Hmmph, yeah, right! My mom would probably throw a fit, though. After all, edges and length are the keys to success according to the Bible of Brenda.

After I hop out of the shower, I walk downstairs so my mom can untwist my hair. My twist out is poppin' and goes perfectly with my "Yasss Queen" tee-shirt that has a picture of who else but Queen Bey on it, which I've paired with a pair of ripped jeans and purple Vans. I grab a breakfast bar and a bottle of water, and just like that, I'm out the door.

"Hey, Ari!" Malia yells at me as she walks out of her house sporting a curly top ponytail shaved in the back with a design and a brand-new retro Steph Curry jersey.

"Hey Lia, that jersey is ice." I say as we walk to the bus.

"Malia Elaine. I know you heard me tell you to put on a jacket!" Ms. Pat, Malia's mom and also the owner of the most dominant all-black law firm in town, yells from the front porch.

"Ma, I'm not cold, and people won't be able to see my jersey." Malia says as she tries to walk quickly to the bus stop. Unfortunately, even the blind, deaf and mute can feel the eyes of Pat Wu searing into their skin. I put my head down and check my nails, which look amazing, btw, and try to appear invisible because I definitely forgot my jacket this morning.

Malia rolls her eyes but knows better and turns around and races back for the jacket her mom is holding and gives her a quick peck on the cheek.

"And don't think I don't see you, Ariana!" she yells at me as she walks back into the house. I roll my eyes and shake my head. Once again, I've been caught by Ms. Pat.

Malia has been my best friend since, well, I don't remember because babies don't know that they have a best friend until someone tells them that's their best friend. So, yeah, Malia and I have been best friends for our entire lives. Malia is tall athletic, with mocha skin and her father's beautiful almond eyes. She's book-smart and street-savvy and loves to play basketball. I know for a fact that she'll be famous one day, and I plan to put her on my client list along with Blue Ivy.

As we wait for the school bus, I tell Malia about my Beyoncé dream.

"Girl, you are so ridiculous. You know there are other people on this earth besides the Carters, right?" She says as she rolls her eyes. "I'm gonna walk you right to Counselor Mohr's office when we get to school because you need help," she laughs as she gets on the bus.

I wave her off and tell her, "Just wait and see, Malia." I shrug my shoulders nonchalantly. "One day, I will be a member of Bey and Ivy's inner circle."

I hop on the bus behind her, throw my rose gold Beats on, and get in Formation.

Today is going to be a good day. I smile.

Chapter 2

Harriet Tubman

"Every great dream begins with a dreamer.
Always remember, you have within you the strength, the patience,
and the passion to reach for the stars to change the world."

- Harriet Tubman.

Harriet Tubman, nicknamed Minty or, as I call her, the 'Mother of Freedom,' was an activist, a survivor, and a feminist. But as I sit here in American History class, I get the glossed-over version of this woman. I raise my hand and try to help my teacher, Miss Culver, a very kind and smart middle-aged woman with so much knowledge of history you can see it coming out of her ears, but just like every other teacher, Miss Culver has to teach to the test—the mysterious test that will somehow decide my future, and decide whether I go to honors A.P., or just sit in a "regular classroom" with "regular people." This same mysterious test will decide my future for me if I'll be going off to community college or Howard.

If you couldn't tell already, I'm completely over the test and all that it stands for.

"Yes, Miss Whitaker?" She acknowledges my hand in her sweet as-honey voice, knowing I'm about to spread the knowledge to the masses.

"Um, yes. So great cliff notes on Harriet T., Miss Culver, but did you also know that H.T. was born not too far away from here, on Maryland's Eastern Shore? And that she made numerous trips to save slaves and her family members, and she NEVER lost a single passenger. But the most interesting and mysterious thing about H.T. was that she suffered from what people thought were seizures, but she claimed were visions straight from God that helped lead her and other slaves to freedom. Now that's what I call a Wonder Woman." I say as I smile and flip my hair. This new hair product is bomb.

Miss Culver, in fact, did know all of the information that I gave her, and her politeness allowed me to go on speaking for five minutes straight. That was until Tyler rudely cut in and asked if we really needed to go in-depth about slavery since it's been over forever. Again, I raise my hand because that's the polite thing to do before I re- educate Tyler on how slavery isn't over and just goes by the new name of mass incarceration. But just as I start to open my mouth to speak, the bell rings loudly, and Tyler is saved, literally, by the bell.

I guess by now, you're wondering who this teenage, Beyoncé loving fashionista, history protégé is. Well, I'm Ariana Rena Whitaker. Daughter of Brenda Verne Whitaker, professor of black history and head of the history department at Howard University, and Calvin

Lee Whitaker, a renowned artist whose collection is presently being exhibited at the African American History Museum, and therefore, I ooze black girl magic with a pinch of sass.

My mom, a short, feisty woman with cinnamon skin and a light peppering of freckles on her face, grew up in the Midwest and came from a typical working middle-class family. Her mother was an accountant, and her father worked in a factory. Her parents wanted better for her, so they put her in predominantly white private schools for her entire educational experience, which makes for a great story of why she's now the head of the history department at Howard, but more on that later.

My father Calvin, a tall Chadwick Bozeman, a.k.a King of Wakanda-looking fella, was adopted by a great couple who couldn't have children. Granddaddy and Mama G were African American artists who taught Art in black community centers for at-risk youth and did side jobs to get by. They allowed my father to find himself through many forms of Art, but once he had the paintbrush in his hand, there was no turning back. It was as if they were meant to be a family, and God plucked his star out of the sky just for them. He grew up in mainly magnet schools geared toward the arts and went to Rhode Island to pursue his art degree and ended up at Howard for a Master's in Art History. I assume you can tell how the story goes. They met in some random history class, and then 4 years later, I came along. Ariana Rena Whitaker, with a face that was molded by my ancestors, with high cheekbones, a wide nose, almond eyes, skin as smooth as silk and the color of ebony. I'm going to guess this ebony skin came from one of my father's biological parents, but you know we come in all different shades of wonderful no matter what the color of our parents.

So there ya have it, folks.

God blessed me with high cheekbones, ebony skin, and a creative and pragmatic mind.

Look at gawd.

Chapter 3

Malia "Not Obama"

It's like Issa Rae followed my mom and dad around when she wrote her story about "Asian bae" and Molly. My mom, Patrice Louise Wu, is annoyingly right all of the time, even when she's not right. My mother grew up amongst the children of diplomats, senators, and privilege. Her mother was the Ambassador to Rwanda, and her father was a high-powered lobbyist; therefore, she is a product of the D.C. elite. She's a lawyer and the owner of a renowned all-black civil rights law firm and has represented and worked with some of the most relevant black people in the world. I won't name-drop, but I will let you know that 44 is her favorite number.

If Shonda Rhimes mixed Olivia Pope with Annalise Keating, her name would be Patrice Wu. She's a tall woman with flawless skin, the body of Michelle O., the brains of Iyanla, and the parental instinct of Claire Huxtable. How my father woo-ed her (pun intended) is beyond me. Philip Wu is a very quiet man with a big laugh.

He's also a judge. His parents are immigrants from the Philippines, who landed in Brooklyn, NY. He's a very unassuming guy with the brain of a genius and the most beautiful almond-shaped eyes; intense, gentle, comforting, and warm all at once.

I'm going to say that's what got Patrice to commit to the only Asian guy at Howard getting his J.D.

Yep, my dad is a Howard grad and proud of it, too!

Like really, really proud—sometimes, even embarrassingly proud, especially during alumni weekends that the Whitakers and us have been attending since before Ari and I were born. I love that my parents are proud HBCU alumni, and without it being said, it's assumed that Ari and I will follow in our parent's footsteps and end up at Howard. Truth be told, I don't know if I'm destined for that kind of life. But like I said, whatever my mom says is right, so I don't really have much of a choice at the moment.

Anyway, I'm Malia Elaine Wu, the daughter of a black elite and a granddaughter of Asian immigrants. I'm the double outsider who gets by on my exotic looks and athletic talent. But at 15, I'm as lost and confused as every other kid trying to figure out their identity and what it means to be a multi-racial child in this world of white privilege and black uprising. I guess I'll find out sooner or later. For now, I'm just taking it slow and easy—one day at a time.

Chapter 4

Thurgood Marshall

"Sometimes history takes things into its own hands."

- Thurgood Marshall.

"Brown vs. Board of Education was the landmark Supreme Court case that ended school segregation in the United States. Hello, this case ended the notion of "Separate but Equal" and is the reason why I'm sitting in class with annoying Tyler. Also, the lead attorney, Thurgood Marshall (another Maryland-born activist) for the plaintiff, would go on to become the first black justice on the United States Supreme Court and a leader in the civil rights movement. Once again, Miss Culver is giving the glossed-over version of this highly important piece of history. I raise my hand and look at Malia, who, of all people, should be raising hers. I eye her, expecting her to raise her hand, but instead, she rolls her eyes at me and sits back in her seat, knowing I'm about to rant away again.

Obviously, Miss Culver knows too, so she politely looks in the other direction and loudly, but still in that sweet voice, says, "This will be your project. You will dissect Brown v. Board of Education and give the positives and negatives and what else you feel needs to happen in the country and more specifically on the educational level to cut the racial divide."

I am as giddy as Beyoncé's gay dancers on a Tuesday. I'm about to death drop right here in this classroom because no one is going to outdo me on this project.

"Also, you will be paired with someone." she continues with the instructions.

"YES! YES! YES", I whisper to myself as I snap my fingers with excitement. "Malia and I are going to kill this project "

"…of my choosing," she says.

"Well damn, Miss Culver!" I think to myself. No, it's okay; Erica or Russell can work this thing out with me, so there's still hope.

"At the end of class, the list will be posted." She ends, then turns toward me and smiles. Her smile bugged me a little. I can't put my head around it; Miss Culver is not really sweet.

For the next thirty minutes, all I can think about is this dope project and how I'm about to kill this thing like Gabby Union. You know that Gabby's style is smart, arrogant, and always on point.

The bell rings, and I jump up to see the posted names. Everyone is moaning, not because of their partners, but because they have no interest in this assignment. I finally get up to the board, entirely too excited to see… "Wait…What?" I say out loud. Malia, who is behind me chatting up Erica and Russell, looks over my shoulder and bursts out laughing. Erica and Russell rush to my side and see the name written next to mine, and they join the laughter. Now everyone is laughing, and it's embarrassing but not more than my partner. He is interested in everything but studies.

"Ughhhhhh…WHY!"

I storm off toward the group of kids sporting Hollister and Sperrys and tap Tyler Manning on the shoulder. He's talking to his "bros," aka the white kids who claim to be color-blind and always have a best friend who's black hidden somewhere in their pockets, I assume. He turns around and gives me a W.T.H. look. So, I fix my face, kinda, and stand up straight.

"I know you probably haven't taken the time to look past your ego at the list, but just so you know, Miss Culver has decided to make us partners for this project, so imma need you to get on your Ps and Qs and make sure you're ready to work or else we can just cut the b.s. now and change partners." I say it politely, well, I tried.

After giving me an agitated look, he turns around to his friends and attempts to make some sly comment, hoping to impress them, but as he turns back around to me, I swing my head and give him all the shade an umbrella can provide and walk back toward my friends who are still laughing.

"Ohhhh, so y'all really think it's funny?"

"Yup." Russell barely gets out as he tries not to double over.

"I'm sorry, girl." Erica says between kee-kees.

"That's what you get for always interrupting Miss Culver." Malia says as she grabs me around my shoulder, halfway trying to console me.

I give them all the side-eye, pretend I'm beyond heated, and walk away.

How can we work together? We are supposed to meet after school, but I am not sure how I am going to handle him and collaborate with him. He's not my cup of tea, and neither am I his cup of tea. If I am a sweet chai latte, he is unsweetened tea. It's not according to my taste buds. It is what the people North of Maryland like. We are total opposites, two far-apart ends of a pole. Even in the cafeteria, we sit at complete opposite corners.

I think Erica and Russell went over to that side of the cafeteria and talked to him and his friends. Erica has this thing for Derrick, so maybe she is trying to get him. And Russell, well, Russell may just want to hang with both the crowds. He's the confused, mixed kid who loves Post Malone but throws Wakanda signs up everywhere we go, but also knows every Maroon 5 and Jay-Z song and doesn't think the country is that bad. Like I said, confused.

Maybe I am just trying to distract myself from the fact that I have to work with Tyler, or perhaps I am fixating too much on it. Anyways, I guess I'll just have to come up with a way to get this project done with Tyler Manning while trying not to lose my sanity.

Chapter 5

Loving v. Virginia

"Love is love is love is love is love is love is love is love:
cannot be killed or swept aside."

- Lin-Manuel Miranda.

I'm Erica Channing. I'm half Trinidadian and half Puerto Rican. My parents were born in the States but refused to give up their island ways and cuisine, so that naturally means that my body refuses to get "American" skinny. But that's okay. I'm a thick girl with straight A's, lashes for days, a head full of fabulous hair, and more than ready to conquer the world. I am confident I can do and get anything I want, but the only thing that's stopping me is… yes! You guessed it: my parents. It is like they have still kept a tight grip on the umbilical cord and separated me. They have to have control over everything that I do. It suffocates me. If only my parents would cut the cord.

My parents, Carlos and Iyana, own a great Caribbean restaurant in the middle of Georgetown, which everyone frequents and raves about. They met when my father walked into my mother's parent's restaurant (yes, the same restaurant) after a long day at class. He saw my mother with her beautiful smile that could light up a room and lashes that fluttered like butterfly wings. My mom was also attending Georgetown, but she worked at her parent's restaurant when she could. They ended up talking about classes and other "stuff" that first night they met. They have been together ever since. Well, I mean, they were young, so I'm sure they broke up every other week as kids do, but now they are married and have one beautiful child and another one I'm supposed to call my brother, Eric Channing.

He's my twin. I try to ignore him as much as possible, but it is difficult because we happen to have the same best friend, Russell Black-Summers, who we grew up with. So I'm stuck hanging out with Eric way more than a sister should ever have to see her sibling.

Anyways, let us get back to me. Right now, I'm in a bit of a bind because I'm in love with this boy named Derrick. Dark hair, light eyes, creamy skin, and a touch of Southern in his voice that makes me melt. He's new to the school, but he hangs out with the Tyler "bros" which annoys the hell out of me. But he's so down to earth that I can't help but fall for him. And luckily, he likes me back. We have reached the talking stage, getting all the rainbows and butterflies. My parents are not aware of this because you know "control" I'm not supposed to be talking to anyone but God and the baby doll I've had since I was three.

It's 2023, and Loving v. Virginia was like fifty years ago, and hello, Barack Obama is mixed, and my parents think he's the greatest thing next to Coquito, but they, mainly my dad, are so traditional that they think I'll find some boy from an island and marry him and inherit the restaurant. Thank goodness I'm only 15 and that school lasts 8 hours a day, so I can talk to Derrick all I want. I know he's the one, so I'll have to tell them someday. Like maybe, the day before the wedding.

Chapter 6

Aretha Franklin

*"We all require and want respect,
man or woman, black or white.
It's our basic human right."*

- Aretha Franklin.

I wake up to Aretha Franklin singing gospel, and it's blaring out of every speaker in the house. I roll over and put the pillow over my head, but I know what today is. It's Saturday, meaning gospel, 90s RnB, and the best of 99 and 2000.

"Dear Lord, why can't I sleep in on a Saturday?

Why?" I mumble to myself.

This has to be considered abuse because, according to studies, teenagers need at least 10 hours of uninterrupted sleep.

Oh well, might as well get up and attempt to be productive. I throw on my Beyoncé Weekend Mix and start cleaning my room, thinking to myself how amazing Aretha Franklin was during the civil rights movement. Most people just know her for her brilliant voice, but she did a lot more. She toured with Dr. Martin Luther King for free to help educate the black community about the civil rights, and funded it with the help of Harry Belafonte. She also hosted many civil rights activists in her home, and most notably, she offered to post bail for Angela Davis, who was considered an enemy of the state at that time but is now one of the most respected activists of our time. But then I think about how she shunned Beyoncé…I guess we are just going to have to agree to disagree on Beyoncé Miss Franklin, but I will always be grateful for your voice and activism.

A few minutes later, my mom walks up the stairs belting "chain, chain, chain," and I know that means she's mad at Dad for something.

She walks into my room, "Hey sweetie, you want to go out to breakfast?"

I respond, "Yesss!" in my Billy Porter voice, drop everything, and hop in the shower.

As I attempt not to get my hair wet because, of course, I forgot to put on my shower cap, I think, "What is Beyoncé doing right this second? Should I order the bacon today or try this vegan thing out again? Do I wear sunglasses and look mysterious, or go without make-up and tell everyone I woke up like this?" So many decisions… Finally, I decided on the bacon and the 'I woke up like this' look. Flawless doesn't happen overnight, my good people.

While I was at breakfast, Russell hit us all up on WhatsApp, asking what everyone was up to today. Malia said she had practiced all day. Erica said she was helping her parents get ready to cater some big shindig at a politician's house, and I replied, "SEND HELP! Mom is playing Aretha!" They all L.O.L.'d and sent GIFs of crazy women. The best one was Angela Bassett standing there with a cigarette and a match while her husband's clothes burned. That was definitely the best part of Waiting to Exhale. They all knew that meant my dad was in trouble and better bring home flowers and compliment my mom on the house being so clean. So Russell saves the day and invites me over to his house to hang out and chill, which is the coolest house in town. His mom, Sara, is obsessed with Frank Lloyd Wright, so she designed a modern version of Falling Waters.

After we finished breakfast, I asked my mom to drop me off there for a few hours. As she dropped me off, she said something weird about how Russell and I better not be 'Netflix and Chilling.'

I replied with a side-eye and an "ew" for so many reasons. Why adults try to use teenage lingo is beyond me.

I jump out of the car, walk up to the front door, and knock. Mrs. Black-Summers answers the door (oh yeah, there are two. I always forget). Mrs. Audra answers the door with her big smile and amazing fro and greets me with a warm hug.

"Hey, Ri-Ri," she says. Mrs. Audra always gives everyone a nickname, whether you like them or not.

"Hi, Mrs. Audra. How are you? Been anywhere interesting lately?".

"Just got back from a trip to L.A., but I'd much rather be in Spain." She says as she walks into her huge open living area.

"Bubs!!! Ri-Ri is here," she yells up towards Russell's room. Russell comes running down the stairs in his Adidas sweatshirt, sweats, and mismatched socks. The mismatched sock thing is his "trademark."

"Hey, Ri-Ri." he chuckles.

"Hey, Bubs." I chuckle back as I stick out my tongue.

I follow him back up to his massive room with every gadget you can think of. As he puts stuff away, I notice Russell has great skin. The color of cream with a splash of coffee, big brown eyes that twinkle even when he's scowling, and a smile as big as Audra's. He's gotten so tall this year and really filled out. When we were little, he was chubby and had cute dimples. But he's really coming into his own now.

"Hey! So, you wanna watch a movie? Mom finally let me jailbreak my fire stick so we can watch anything that's at the movie theatre, or we can just chill." He says while looking around aimlessly for something.

Wait, did he just try to ask me if I wanted to "fire stick and chill." No! Russell is not that kind of guy, and anyway, he's my best friend.

"Sure, how about we watch Blackkklansman." I reply. So he finds it, and we both plop into his oversized beanbags and really just chill.

Chapter 7

M.L.K., Jr.

"Injustice anywhere is a threat to justice everywhere."

- Dr. Martin Luther King, Jr. ,
Letter from Birmingham Jail.

How many times do we have to hear the same "I Have a Dream Speech?" I think, which Tyler says aloud.

"Excuse me, Miss Culver." I raise my hand and give Tyler the side-eye.

"Yes, Miss Whitaker?" she smiles, but her voice isn't as sweet as usual, but I ignore it and continue.

"Miss Culver, do you think maybe we could listen to the Letters from Birmingham Jail instead? We've all memorized this speech because we've all been hearing it since pre-school." Well, I'm pretty sure my mom played it on those belly buds while I was in the womb, but that's neither here nor there.

"I think that's a great idea, Miss Whitaker." As she stops I Have a Dream and starts Letters from Birmingham Jail.

The Letters from Birmingham Jail was a series of letters written and combined into one document, written by Dr. King in response to white ministers releasing an open letter to him in the.

Birmingham newspaper while he was in jail, which criticized him and his protests to the ongoing racial inequality and violence towards blacks in Birmingham. Though the copy of the letter never actually made it to the ministers, it became a rallying cry for the civil rights movement, demanding that people stop passively watching the injustices, stand up, and fight for equality and justice for all.

I listen intently while Malia passes love notes back and forth with Cai, Erica keeps making eyes with Derrick, and Russell tries to listen, but Tyler is bugging him about soccer practice. Russell is a good kid. Comes from a good family. His mom is a lawyer who works with Malia's mom, and his other mom is an architect at a large firm in the suburbs. He is kind, funny, and smart— but hates when you call him any of those things. He's shy for no reason, which is the opposite of me, but he has the best jokes and the cutest dimples. Too bad he hangs out with Tyler when he's not hanging out with Eric and us. The speech ends right as the bell rings.

"We will discuss this tomorrow, so I hope you all listened." Miss Culver yells as everyone rushes out to lunch.

Chapter 8

Drake by Day, Aubrey by Night

*"Sometimes, it's the journey
that teaches you a lot about your destination."*

- Drake, aka Aubrey Graham.

I'm Russell Black-Summers. I come from the all-American dream. I have two wonderful parents with post-graduate degrees, living successful lives and raising their gifted son in the suburbs of D.C. We have one dog, one cat, five fishes, and my grandmother, Nina.

My mother, fondly known as Mama Audra, is a lawyer and an ex-collegiate basketball player for Georgetown. She is also what you call a jack-of-all-trades. Like the civil rights activist Angela Davis, Audra is African-American and has a fiery, outspoken personality. After attending Howard Law but before deciding to practice law, she decided to coach and travel the world as a flight attendant while I was still young, so we've been all over the world in my 15 years. My other mother, Sara, on the other hand, is white and hails from a rural Midwestern farm town. She is an architect. She's the more "settled" of the two. My mom, Sara, would rather stay home and garden than go on whirlwind trips. She fell in love with my mom but may not have fully understood the situation she was getting herself into. Despite their constant loud.

"Discussions," as my mother likes to call them, they somehow manage to make it work.

Long story short, Ms. Pat called my mama and told her to get her head out of the clouds and come back down to earth so she could help her save the world from injustice. So that's what she did. She put in her resignation and partnered with Ms. Pat at Wu, Black-Summers, King, and Associates; they run the most well-known civil rights law firm in D.C.

Some days, my mama is on cloud nine defending the defenseless, the people who nobody wants to defend. But I think she just wants to be back up in the clouds. My mom, Sara, on the other hand, is just happy we are all home together.

Mom constructed Nina a mother-in-law suite so that she could have a separate living space and avoid the noise and activity of the main house. And she is happy about it. I believe that Nina enjoys drinking her wine in a serene environment, free from any criticism or scrutiny.

I sometimes find myself divided between two worlds. It is as if I don't know who I am anymore; am I white, or am I black? I frequently contemplate whether I should align myself with a particular group, but my mother consistently advises me that neither side is superior and that I should embrace my identity. I view us as a team with diverse perspectives and unique qualities united in our shared objectives. I have an affection for those eccentric women. I also have great admiration for.

Ariana, but unfortunately, she is unaware of it. It seems that unless the topic revolves around Beyoncé or social justice, she is not interested in engaging in conversation. I will wait patiently until she realizes it.

Chapter 9

Biggie Smalls: "Mo' money Mo' problems"

"We can't change the world unless we change ourselves."

- Notorious B.I.G

So, like I said, I have to figure out a way to do this project with Tyler. So, at lunch, I walk over to his table. "Hey, Tyler. Do you have a sec? When do you think you'll be available to do our project." I say with a fake smile.

He looks over his shoulder and says, "Sure, how about my house after school? You know where I live." as he continues his conversation with his bros.

"Yup." I clench my teeth and walk away.

Everyone knows where Tyler lives. He has the biggest house in the school. His dad is a Democratic senator from Connecticut, just like his dad before him. Senator Manning talks a great game for justice and equal rights and being color-blind but bathes in white privilege, and it has been passed down to his son. He and Malia's mom went to school together. They grew up amongst the same bougie people. So, we get to hear funny stories about Senator Manning that remind us of his son Tyler. Let's.

just say thank goodness social media wasn't big back in their day.

I see my mom pulling up after school in Shelly O., her ode to Mrs. Obama, and a present to herself when she was named the head of the History Department. A smooth black Mercedes with sleek features and a powerful engine. Now, you would think she would be dressed to match this car, but when I peek in, she has a head scarf, an India Arie tee shirt, some African print pants, and her faithful Birkenstocks (those shoes are almost as old as I am). She doesn't care though, like, she tells me, "She ain't her hair," or her car for that matter, and that is why I love me some Brenda!

As we drive to Tyler's house, I tell her about how I'm dreading it and all the uneducated stuff Tyler says.

"Listen, baby cakes, the only way to learn something is to go to the source and to ask questions. He may feel insecure, and that's why he says that stuff. I have learned that with my students, it has to be a judgment-free zone so that ideas, opinions, and, most importantly, facts can freely flow." She says, sounding all Maya Angelou.

"I know, Mom, but he just gets on my nerves." I responded, not wanting to hear her.

"Well, go in there and get this done. I'll be back in 2 hours to get you. Text me if anything comes up." she replies, kissing me on the cheek.

"Okay. Maybe just drive around the block," I say, halfway serious.

She laughs and unlocks the door, so I hop out. I ring the doorbell. Mrs. Manning, Tyler's mom, answers the door. She has the most beautiful auburn hair with a hint of honey and striking green eyes. She is the epitome of a senator's wife. She's all decked out in her Eileen Fisher, which she considers loungewear, and welcomes me into their massive foyer.

"Hi, Mrs. Manning. How have you been?" I say.

"I'm doing well, Ari. How are your parents?" She says as she flashes the biggest yellow diamond I've ever seen hanging from her neck.

"Damnnnnn, Mrs. Manning." I think to myself as I'm being blinded. Did I mention that Mrs. Manning loves American Art, and she owns pieces from my dad's collection that she loves to brag about?

"They are great! Just working a lot. My dad should be getting back from Italy today or tomorrow," I say, looking around at all of the beautiful art in the space.

"How wonderful. Say hello to your dad for me, and tell him that I'm waiting for him to sell that piece at the museum." She replies as she walks toward the bottom of the dual staircase. You know, the fancy kind from Cinderella (The Brandy and Whitney one…).

"Tyler, Ari's here!" She yells into oblivion.

Now we have a nice size house, and I'm not complaining or even Jonesing, but lawd, this thing is just ridiculous. Tyler comes running downstairs decked out in all Nike (yeah, right! like he's supporting Kap) with his perfectly gelled hair and eyes the color of the Mediterranean ocean.

"Hey, Ari." he says all nonchalantly.

"Hey, Tyler." I say, disinterested.

"Well, I'll leave you two kids to it then. Nice seeing you, Ari." Mrs. Manning says as she walks out of the room.

I follow Tyler into his library. He points out where his father told him he could find old law books, and I go over to the library and admire all of the old bindings of history.

"Wow, this is awesome, Tyler." I say with genuine excitement.

"Yeah, I guess." he says as he shrugs his shoulders.

I pull out an old con-law book that has the Brown v. Board of Education case in it and start reading. I don't understand one bit of it besides the synopsis, which, fortunately, I already knew. Tyler sits there playing with his Apple Watch, totally uninterested.

"Listen, Tyler, I want to do really well on this project, and if you're not willing to put in the work, then let me know now so we can do it separately.".

He looks up at me and frowns. "Listen, Ariana..." he says to me in a snarky voice. "It makes no sense why we keep having to go over this stuff when I sit in a classroom with you, and my best friend is literally black."

"We have accomplished the dream, and racism is pretty much null and void except for a few crazies out there. But we can't change them." He says arrogantly as if he has just solved the Da Vinci code by claiming a black best friend.

My head snaps back in disbelief. I think to myself, do we not watch the same news? Do the news and posts about racism that appear on my Facebook timeline not appear on his? Is he that white privileged?

"Oh really!" is all I could say because I was trying to stay right with God and my ancestors.

I pack up my things and walk out without a word. Tyler stares at me dumbfounded but doesn't say anything or make a move.

"Bye, Mrs. Manning." I say as I walk toward the door.

"Oh? That was quick; everything okay?" She says, looking confused.

"Yeah. Everything is great. I just came over to pick up a book, and we will meet again later." I say as I shut the door.

I take a deep breath and think to myself as I pace back and forth in front of his gates because I remembered that I'm across town, so I had to text my mom to come back, hoping she took my advice and just drove around the block. How could someone who has parents who are so liberal be so oblivious to what's going on in the world?

Chapter 10

Justin Timberlake: "Say Something..."

"Burying black people out of sight and out of mind while extracting our culture, our dollars, our entertainment like oil — black gold, ghettoizing and demeaning our creations, then stealing them, gentrifying our genius and then trying us on like costumes before discarding our bodies like rinds of strange fruit."

- Jesse Williams, 2016 BET Awards speech.

As I watch Ariana walk out, I'm super confused and annoyed. Why does everything have to be about race, and why is she always so damn sensitive. She has the same privileges as I do. She lives in a big house with highly successful parents and goes to the same expensive ass school as me. So why am I always at fault for something? How is it possible that I'm so privileged if she has the same stuff that I have? If I'm joking, I'm insensitive. If I'm serious, I'm uneducated and naive, or my white privilege is showing. I have no clue how to handle her.

It's not my fault that my dad is a senator. Who, by the way, is a Democrat and is constantly making speeches about equal rights and justice for all. Devoting most of his campaign to the causes Ari speaks about. Also, my mom.

has done great things for women and women's rights, and she's even collaborated with H.R.C.

I come from a progressive family, and I consider myself to be a liberal. Just because I don't go around saying Black Lives Matter and protest doesn't mean I don't believe in those things. Shoot, I think I'm more progressive than them. I would have voted for Bernie. I'm 15, for crying out loud. I just want to do well enough to get into an Ivy League and play soccer so my parents will be proud of me. I don't see color. But even when I say that, Ari rolls her eyes, and Russell elbows me in the side to shut up. I just can't win.

For instance, my favorite music is rap and a little E.D.M., I support Kap, and Lebron is my favorite athlete. Like, hello, how could I possibly be racist? I'm like the J.T. of R.B.G. I love everyone, no matter their color. I'm all about the blurred lines. It's what makes this country so great.

Let's hope Ari and I can make it through this project together because, at this point, it's not looking so good. I actually really respect Ariana and think she's the smartest girl in history, and most of the time, my comments are to rile her up, but I guess I went too far this time, so I'll make sure to apologize when I see her tomorrow.

Chapter 11

Lena Waithe

"You can talk all day long,
but if you don't do something, it's a waste."

- Lena Waithe.

You know Lena had it right. Bide your time and wait for the perfect moment, like your homeboy getting in trouble for being a creeper, and then show the world your greatness. I woke up this morning and decided I was going to run for Sophomore Class President. We have the election right around midterms during the first semester. Last year, Michaela Stone won because she was the most popular girl in our 8th-grade class and is literally involved in everything that's "cool." But this is my year; I can feel it.

As I walk into school, "Ego" blasting in my ears, I take my Beats off and puff my hair back out. Today, I'm sporting a wash and go along with a T.L.C.-inspired 90s look. My mom helped me find a vintage t-shirt with Lisa "left-eye" Lopez on it; it says "No Scrubs." We went and found some jeans called JNCOs that are really big but totally make the outfit with a pair of purple combat boots. I'm feeling myself.

"I'm running for class president," I say to Malia.

"Cool. Cool. You should totally do it," she says while texting Cai, obviously not interested in my revelation.

"Hey, do you like my outfit?" She asks once she's done being preoccupied.

Today, she's sporting a retro Jordan Wizards Jersey, black jeans, and low black on black #9s.

"Yeah, they look dope, and I see you came through drippin' with those new earrings." Both were diamond-encrusted 3s for her basketball number 33.

Malia has swag; that's probably why we are best friends, besides the fact that she's the keeper of my secrets and deals with my crazy. She's super pretty but not in a show-off kind of way; she's just cool.

We keep chatting as we walk to class, and before stepping into history, Tyler pulls me to the side. "Ughhhh, will he just ever go away." I think to myself as I snatch my arm away and give him my best resting bitch face (RBF).

"Hey, listen, I was a jerk yesterday. How about I come over to your house after school one day this week, and we'll try it again? I need to do well on this project too." he says, actually looking slightly genuine.

"Sure." I say as I push past him and go grab a seat between Russell, who is sporting a fresh faux-hawk with 2 lines on the side, and Erica, who looks perplexed about a text.

I tap Erica on the arm and say, "Hey, chica, what's up with the look?"

"Oh, nothing. Just trying to figure out who this girl is on Derrick's Snapchat." she says.

I lean over and see an average-looking brunette with her arms wrapped around a smiling Derrick.

"Who is this "Becky" with the long hair?" I say, looking super offended for my friend.

"I don't know, but you know I'm about to find out." she replies as she walks off.

It's very weird because when Erica gets upset, she gets the slightest hint of a Caribbean accent, but the thing is, Erica was born and raised in the District. It must be her ancestors rising up from the dead because I'm telling you, that accent is real and scary A.F.

Chapter 12

Shawn Carter meets Solange Knowles

*"What I'm trying to say to girls
is don't let these guys in your head."*

- Cardi B.

As soon as the bell rings to dismiss us from school, I see Derrick walking up to Erica.

"E! Why have you been ghosting me all day?" He asks as he catches up to us.

Erica looks him in the eye and says with that Caribbean accent, "Why don't you ask Becky."

"Who's Becky?" he replies with a flustered and sincerely confused look.

I immediately step in-between the two like Solange in the elevator, ready to flex on sweet Derrick. I throw my phone in Derrick's face and show him the picture on Snap.

Side note: Always have receipts.

He looks at the picture and laughs. I don't see anything funny about the situation.

"Seriously?" He says. "That's my cousin, Joy. She came up to visit from Richmond. Don't you remember me telling you my family was coming up?"

"Oh." I say as I pull the phone away quickly and look over at Erica, who's still scowling at him.

"Oh, okay, but I still don't find it funny." She replies and starts to walk off.

Another side note: make sure the receipts are correct.

Derrick grabs Erica by the waist, pulls her close, and says in that soft southern voice that could melt butter, "Babe, there's no one in this world for me except you...oh, and maybe the older sister from Black-ish."

Erica pops him in the chest, and he laughs while he rubs his chest.

"Just kidding, you're it for me." he says, pulling her in and kissing her.

"I better be!" She replies and smiles as she cuddles him closer.

Those two are Crazy in Love. I don't know more of which, but they are happy. And I'm just happy I didn't have to go full Solange on poor Derrick.

Chapter 13

Shirley Chisholm

"If they don't give you a seat at the table, bring a folding chair."

- Shirley Chilsom.

"Sooooo, this morning I decided I'm going to run for class president." I say while downing Dad's famous lasagna.

"That's great, sweetie!" my mom says as she sips the vintage Italian wine my dad brought back from his trip.

"I figure there are no spies lurking around my school, so I'll have a pretty decent chance at winning." I say as I think about the new kid who just started school last week. What was his name again?

"Well, I think it's great!" My mom says, "You know Shirley Chisholm was the first black woman elected to Congress and the first to run for President of the United States. She was a bold and brilliant feminist who faced harsh criticism and discrimination during her political career, but her biography *Unbought and Unbossed* says it all. I'll have to see if I can find it for you. It's a very inspiring book. Oh, and she had true diva style!".

Perfect, I thought. I definitely have style going for me, then. Now, I just have to figure out what the people of Ruth Bader Ginsburg Prep need and want.

We finish dinner, and it's my night to do the dishes. I hear smooth jazz playing on the speakers, peek around the corner, and watch my mom and dad cuddle up in the nook of the couch with their red wine. They are definitely #relationshipgoals.

I head upstairs and research Ms. Chisholm to make sure I'm prepared for the fight and try to come up with a slogan since "Yes We Can" and "Stronger Together" have already been used. I'm sure Queen Bey will give me some inspiration.

"Alexa, please play my Black Girl Magic Mix." I say as I sit on my bed and daydream.

Chapter 14

Janelle Monae

"Embrace what makes you unique, even if it makes others uncomfortable. I didn't have to become perfect because I've learned throughout my journey that perfection is the enemy of greatness."

- Janelle Monae.

Besides trying to be the first black woman for President, I also live for fashion. I have found inspiration in every era and century, from the cat eye of Cleopatra, the African queen, not Elizabeth Taylor, to Janelle Monae, who has mastered androgyny and femininity and managed to make it an all-inclusive look.

Yesterday, my mom took me to get a blowout, so I'm rocking a high ponytail that feels like silk and swings like Oprah's hair in the 90s. I decided to rock a cute red blazer with a 2-Pac tee shirt, black jeans, cat-eye glasses inspired by Miss Chisolm, and knee-high boots.

"Okay...I see you, Willow Smith." Malia says to me as she walks up, swinging her head back and forth, sporting her new Miami Heat jersey in the Miami Vice colors and some cool Nike IDs to match.

"Okay, Miss Wade," I reply back.

We walk to the bus stop together, chatting about our weekend. I spent mine making posters with my dad before he left for his next trip, and Malia spent hers hanging out with Cai and playing in a basketball tournament.

"Don't you ever get sad that your dad is gone so much?" Malia asks me.

"Yeah. But I'm used to it, and he's living his dream and showing me that striving for greatness is okay," I reply.

"As long as my mom's okay with it. I'm cool." I say, wondering if my mom is actually okay with it.

I immediately shake off that weird feeling and look up from the phone after admiring Beyoncé on Instagram. Today, she is standing in a random hallway in a floral print freakum dress, looking disinterested yet completely infatuated. How in the world does she pull off that look?

"So, do you want to be my campaign manager or nah?" I ask Malia as we ride to school.

"I thought you'd never ask." She replies as she rolls her eyes, looks back at her phone, and starts texting someone who's obviously more important than me at the moment.

"Fine, never mind! I'll ask Russell. He's always down for the cause." I say, putting my Beats on and bobbing my head to "Diva.".

"Hey," Russell says as he waits for us to walk up to school. Side note: his mom won't let him ride the bus because Russell is a delicate flower that will be wilted by the drama of teen gossip. Honestly, I think his grandma just likes to drive him so she can hear all the latest gossip.

"Your outfit is fiyah, Ari." he says, giving me that million-watt smile.

"Thanks," I say as I twirl for the full effect. "I'm announcing I'm running for class president today, so I wanted to give the children Sasha Fierce.

"Cool," he says. "Let me know if you need any help."

"As a matter of fact, I need a campaign manager." I say as I give Malia the side-eye. She ignores me and continues to text Cai.

"I'm down, just let me know what you need," he says.

"Thanks, Russell. I can always count on you." I say to him while shooting laser beams in Malia's direction.

"Bet. You know I'm always here," he says, and I feel a little tingle in my stomach.

Malia rolls her eyes as we walk into class.

Chapter 15

Colin Kaepernick

"I'm for truth, no matter who tells it. I'm for justice no matter who's against it."

- Malcolm X.

While I'm consumed with the thought of starting my own revolution at RBG Prep, Miss Culver drones on about mediocre facts about the Civil Rights Movement. Man, I wish she would get deeper because there are so many pivotal moments that happened during that time.

"So, who do you see as the present-day Malcolm X." Miss Culver asks.

"I would say Colin Kaepernick." Tyler says without raising his hand. My head snaps up, waiting for him to make some ignorant comment, but Miss Culver redirects the conversation into something meaningful.

Okay, I see you, Miss Culver! Down for the cause! I think to myself.

That was actually a really good answer, even if it was Tyler who said it. Who is the Malcolm X of our generation? Kap started a great dialogue that has been plagued with misinformation and ignorance. It's always funny to me that people go directly to race when wanting to confront an issue that deals with oppression and.

inequality more than the actual issue of race. Colin, like Obama, is a mixed kid raised by a white woman. So why do people immediately take a piece of someone's identity to dehumanize them? I don't know if we will ever know the answer, but I'll keep searching until I find out.

"Ari!" Tyler yells from behind me. "I'll be over at your house around 4, okay?"

"Yeah, that's fine!" I yell back over my shoulder and go and find my Crew. Erica is looking extra Lupita today in her long African skirt, tank top, and a head full of curls.

"Wakanda Forever." I say and sign to her as I walk up.

She smiles and starts telling me about her weekend and how she was trying to sneak to the movies with Derrick, but her parents told her she and her brother needed to help them prepare for Carnival. As she's going on about, Derrick Russell walks up dressed in his soccer uni, looking like David Beckham and Idris Elba's love child.

Is he growing facial hair?

Malia interrupts my train of thought when she walks up.

"Hey, do you guys want to skip lunch at school and go to Shake Shack?" She says with a mischievous smile on her face.

We all raise our hands with a resounding "YES."

Chapter 16

Nina Simone

"There's no excuse for the young people not knowing who the heroes and heroines are or were."

- Nina Simone.

As we walk out of school, Russell's Grandma, Nina, pulls up in her red Cadillac SUV, rocking salt and pepper locs and some fierce Jackie- O sunglasses, looking like the opposite of secret service, but hey, she's sneaking us to Shake Shack so I'm in. Nina is the dopiest grandma on this earth. She can either find her listening to Nina Simone or Kanye West, pre-Kardashian, of course.

Today, she picks us up, blasting To Be Young, Gifted, and Black.

"Hey, Nina," Russell says as he greets her with a kiss on the cheek. "Thanks for picking us up."

"No problem, just don't tell your parents, or they will all have my neck." She laughs and drives off.

This song by Nina Simone was a tribute to the black youth of the 1960s who were treated as less than their white counterparts and were made to feel is if they weren't apart of the so-called American Dream. Little did they know they were their ancestor's wildest dreams. This song still resonates today with the various forms of violence in and against the black community and unequal educational opportunities. Nina turns up the volume during the best part of the song, and we all sing along; "In the whole world, you know, there's a million boys and girls who are YOUNG, GIFTED, and BLACK.

And that's a FACT."

I love Nina because she's not afraid to talk about politics or other social issues affecting our community or the world. She is always willing to listen to our side without judgment.

After we each order our favorite burgers, milkshakes, and fries, we all sit down and start talking about what happened over the weekend.

I interrupt, "Okay, so today, when we get back, I plan to announce that I'm running for class president. I haven't decided if I should do it right after the gym when we are lining up or right after Geometry before the last bell rings. Any thoughts?"

"I think you should definitely do it after gym— more people will be able to spread the word that way." Erica replies.

"True. So after gym, it is!" I say with a big smile on my face.

"I think it's great you're running for President, Ari. That school needs a little more flavor, if you ask me. America should know by now to trust black women." chimed in Nina. We all laugh and finish our lunch. Yup, a little flavor never hurt anyone, and that's a FACT.

Chapter 17

Venus & Serena

"You have to let fear go. Another lesson is you just have to believe in yourself; you just have to. There's no way around it. No matter how things are stacked against you, you just have to every time."

- Venus Williams.

As I sat down to lunch with my best friend Malia, I couldn't help but notice that something was off. Malia, who's known for her quick wit and smart-ass comments, was uncharacteristically gloomy.

Sensing something was amiss, I asked, "Hey Lia, what's up with you?"

"Nothing. Cai is just acting funny," she replied, her voice tinged with sadness.

I wanted to help her, to be there for her, but I didn't know how. So, I did what any good friend would do - I offered her my support.

"Well, if you want to talk about it, you know I'm here." I said, nudging her with my shoulder.

Malia smiled weakly. "Thanks. Maybe later. Now let's go show these chicks what the Williams sisters' third cousins can do." she said, trying to lighten the mood.

I followed her outside to the tennis courts, feeling a mixture of worry and excitement. Malia was my best friend, and I hated seeing her upset. But at the same time, I was pumped up for tennis - those lessons my mom had put me in until 5th grade had paid off, and I was ready to show off my skills.

As we walked, thoughts of Malia's girlfriend, Cai Johnson, kept nagging at me. Cai was the star track runner at our school, and she came from a family of track stars. With his tall, lean frame, cocoa skin, and light brown eyes, he was every bit the athlete you'd expect. But she was more than that to Malia.

I really liked them together. It was like something out of a corny teen movie - the star basketball player dating the school's track star. They fit together perfectly, and I couldn't help but feel a little envious of their love. The only issue was that no one knew they were together. Well, no one except the Crew, our close-knit group of friends. But that was it. They hadn't come out to anyone else, and I knew why.

They were gay. And in our community, that was still a big deal. Malia and Cai weren't ready to deal with the backlash from their families and the rest of the community. They weren't ready to deal with the prejudice and judgment that came with it.

It was tough being powerful, beautiful, and talented. I hoped Malia and Cai would figure out that they were great no matter who they loved. No matter the cost, they would have the courage to come out and be their true selves.

As we stepped onto the courts, I took a deep breath. I was ready to play my heart out. And I was ready to be there for Malia, no matter what.

Chapter 18

Stacy Abrams

"Not everyone's ambitions will be world domination or Carnegie Hall,
but we should be driven beyond
what we know and feel safe doing."

- Stacy Abrams.

The underdog always has the best story. The amazingly talented and resilient Georgia leader has been my inspiration since the first time I saw her on YouTube. Not only is she a fierce advocate for voters' rights (and should have been the governor of Georgia, she is a romance author. Okay Ms. Abrams, all is fair in love and politics. And that's how I like to think of myself. I don't fit the stereotype and have no desire to.

"Mhmm." I clear my throat as I stand on the bleachers. "Hey, everyone!" I say, obviously not loud enough because everyone is still chatting and on their phones. "Mhmmm." I clear my throat again, loud enough this time. "HEY!" I yell, and everyone looks up (awkward, but go with it).

"So, Hi, I'm Ariana Whitaker, and I'm running for Sophomore Class President." It sounds more like a question than a statement, but I just keep chugging along. "I want to bring something different to RBG Prep.

leadership. I feel like we have the potential to do something great because of our diversity and commitment to inclusivity (a big word I found while researching Stacy). Anyway...thank you for your attention. Please let me know the areas in which you would like to see improvement in our school. I would greatly appreciate your vote in the upcoming election."

"Ari Whitaker, Cuz I'm ready to 'Slay and get in Formation' for the students of RBG Prep." I say with a big smile (okay, it's not the best slogan, but hey, Yonce hasn't failed me yet).

A few people clap, and Malia hits me with an "okkkkurrrr," but most people just go back to using their phones.

I step off of the bleachers, shaking my head, "See this voter apathy. That's why we had that orange dude in the office." I say as I throw my hand up in the air.

Malia puts her arm around me as we walk out of the gym, "Great slogan. I know you're totally going to slay once you prez," she says as she hugs me tighter.

That's what best friends are for, I think to myself.

Malia will always be my number-one hype man.

Chapter 19

Prince

"You can always tell if the groove is working or not."

- Prince.

As the distinct sound of knocking reverberated through the air, I was jolted out of my focused research of Michelle Obama's speeches. Dang, is it 4 already? As I make my way to the door, my mind still lingering on the unfinished task at hand, I say a short prayer that this meeting is better than the first one and that I don't have to kick Tyler's behind out of my crib.

As I open the door, I am greeted by the sight of Tyler, standing there in his navy-blue Vineyard Vines pull-over, jeans, and Cole Haan Oxfords. His preppy modelesque appearance was cute or whatever. No cap, I couldn't help but appreciate his effortless sense of style.

"Hey," he says, almost with a twinge of nervousness.

"Hey," I reply. "Come on in," I say as I lead him back to my mom's study.

The study room is a tribute to the legendary musician Prince; my mom is a huge fan. The walls of the room are painted a vibrant purple, with oversized chairs that are upholstered in matching purple velvet. A.

collection of Prince's albums is displayed prominently on the walls, while a selection of his concert tickets is framed and scattered throughout the room. While some may describe the decor as being on the obsessive side, the owner of the room insists that the environment is conducive to her creativity and productivity. However, for some, the overwhelming use of the color purple may prove to be a bit overwhelming and headache-inducing.

The look on Tyler's face is priceless. It's kind of panicked yet intriguing.

"My mom loves Prince and swears he was like a walking prophet, hence the room," I say, shaking my head.

"I see…" he says, looking around, not quite sure where to sit.

"Anyway, she has some history books with info on the civil rights movement during the time of B v. B, so we can start researching what was going on," I say, trying to change the subject.

"Okay. Cool." Tyler replies as he pulls out his MacBook with a Bernie Bro sticker stuck on the top and sits down in one of the oversized purple velvet chairs.

Even though I'm still with her, this might work out after all; I think to myself as I take a seat next to the raspberry beret on display.

Chapter 20

Rashida Jones

"I believe race is too heavy a burden to carry into the 21st century. It is time to lay it down. We all came here in different ships, but now we're all in the same boat."

- Former Congressman and Civil Rights leader John Lewis.

Teachers, while providing invaluable services to students, often go unnoticed. Despite our critical role in educating and nurturing your children, many are unaware of our backgrounds or origins. As educators, we remain committed to excellence, even if our efforts may go unnoticed.

My name is Anita Culver, the daughter of a midwife and a historian. My mother was the complexion of Dorothy Dandridge, and my father looked like the handsome Harry Belafonte, so needless to say, they were both fair with Caucasian-leaning features. Therefore, I came out with skin the color of toasted ivory, a pointed nose, easily straightened hair, and curious brown eyes. Everyone I meet always assumes I'm white or non-descript before they ever get to know me, even my own students. I'm kind of like the Rashida Jones of teaching, except my father isn't the most well-known musical composer on the earth.

Anyway, I was born and raised in Baltimore, right at the tail end of the civil rights movement. My parents were huge supporters of the movement but never really spoke to me about it while I was growing up, so I took it upon myself to research African American History and was completely mesmerized by the beauty and the tragedy of the time. I'm an eternal optimist who believes and hopes that my classes will understand the importance of American History and realize that African American History is a part of everyone's history and not just exclusively an African American issue. Hopefully, the world will eventually be a better place. Therefore, each year, I give my students a group project on the civil rights movement and force them to be uncomfortable with the realization that racism still exists but the hope that they can change it one day.

Chapter 21

Bernie Sanders

"Difficult times often bring out the best in people."

- Bernie Sanders.

People argue back and forth whether Bernie Sanders and his Bros are good for the "black cause." I do give Mr. Sanders cool points because he did go on freedom rides and marched in the 60s during the civil rights movement. He has some progressive ideas that lots of young people can get behind. However, he's still an old white man who just seems super angry, and he's making his young white male followers super annoying to be around.

As I walk through the halls with Erica, I see different posters of people running for class leadership positions. Everyone's posters seem aight, but I guess they don't have an artist helping them out, so I'll give them a pass.

"Girl, I hope you win this election so you can be on the Winter Social committee." Erica says as she texts Derrick.

"Last year was whack, and I cannot take another Taylor Swift and Shawn Mendes mixtape." She looks up and gives me a serious look.

"I hope I win, too!" I say, super excited and then super disappointed as I spot that a Tyler Bro has decided to run against me. His sign says, "Free Soda, Free kale Chips, Free Beats earbuds (just kidding)." Basically, he wants to socialize the school vending machines. I roll my eyes and keep it moving. I highly doubt Principal Markowitz is going for that.

The Winter Social is the biggest dance of the year for underclassmen. We get to design the entire thing from top to bottom, and if you make the head of the committee, you get to choose the most important thing of the night: MUSIC. We already know that Beyoncé and the entire Carter Family will be bumping the speakers.

I think I just figured out my victory song, "Who Run The World? ...GIRLS".

I got this thing in the bag!

Chapter 22

Bend It Like Beckham

"Hurry up, or we are going to be late for Russell's game." I say as Malia clicks through my various Beyonce playlists (there are many) and Erica rummages through my closet. "Ariana, can I borrow this for the game?" Erica says as she pulls out a shirt that I don't think will accommodate all of her goodies. Gosh, how did she get so lucky-I'm barely working with a B. "Sure, go for it, girl." I say—knowing she will change 3 more times in the next 5 minutes.

"How cool is that Russell and Derrick…and Tyler are starting against S&F." Malia says as she starts to put her KD's on—which are so cute—they are the school colors Red, White, and Blue with a Crown on top of the letters RBG.

"I hope we get them back because they whooped up last year." I say as I put on some cute earrings I found on Etsy that look like RBG dissenter collars and throw on my school tee, a cute pair of joggers and my red air maxes with stars and stripes shoe laces.

"I can't wait to see Derrick out there. He is so darn cute in his soccer uniform," Erica says as she throws off the shirt she just asked to wear and settles for one of the.

school shirts I had made with Justice Ginsburg sporting a crown like Biggie Smalls.

"Ladies, are you ready?" My mom yells from the bottom of the stairs.

We check ourselves out one last time in my oversized mirror that I begged for Christmas and walk down the stairs.

"Hey, Destiny's Child…" My mom says as we file down the stairs looking extra cute. I'm Beyonce, of course—even though I have about as much rhythm as Michelle. But I have Sasha Fierce in my blood, so I still get to claim Bey.

As my mom drops us off at the match, she says something about being behind the bleachers. We all give her a crazy look as we get out and say goodbye. Where does this woman get this stuff from?

"Go, Russell!" I yell as he dribbles the ball down and passes it off to Tyler. Tyler makes some amazing moves and hits Russell with the crazy pass, and Russell hits a header into the net. The crowd goes wild, and we end up winning 2-1. GO, DISSENTERS!

"Hey." Tyler says as he walks up to me.

"Hey." I say. "Good game!"

"Thanks," he replies. "Maybe you should come to every game." he says as he gives me a side smile.

"Hey!" Russell says as he walks up from behind me and puts his hand on my shoulder.

"Hey!" I say to him, and for some reason, blush. Thank goodness for this ebony skin. "Great game." I say as I awkwardly tap on the arm.

"Thanks." he says and flashes me a killer smile.

"So, who's hungry." Derrick says as he walks up from behind the bleachers with Erica, who is beaming.

"I was…" Malia says as she gives everyone a disgusted look.

"Shake Shack?" I suggest. Everyone says yes, and we file off to get in cars.

As Malia and I jump back into my mom's car, she looks at me and shakes her head, chuckling because she can see my confused look.

"What?" I say.

"Nada." she replies and laughs.

"I'm gonna fight you, girl." I say, pushing her into the door.

"Okay. Bet…" she says, giving me a knowing look. I just look away until we get to Shake Shack.

Chapter 23

Whitney Houston

"I'm a person who has life and wants to live, and always have."

- Whitney Houston.

It's the anniversary of Whitney Houston's death, which also happens to be my parent's anniversary, so needless to say, my mother and I are in mourning. Dad called to make sure Mom got the flowers; he was super sweet and also sent me chocolates because he knows my love for Whitney is deep. OMG, what will I do if Beyoncé goes before me? No, no, no, Queen Bey's blood is blessed by the voodoo priestesses of Louisiana, so she will live forever.

I'm lying across my bed when I hear a light tap on the door. I tell whoever is there to hold because the best part of "I will always love you" is about to hit, and I need alone time and focus in order to hit that note (Ok, I didn't hit the note, but it felt good). You know that Whitney Houston bridged the gap between pop and RnB. Without Whitney, there would be no Pink, Justin Timberlake, or Bruno Mars. She is the queen of Pop and always will be.

"Come in." I say with gloom in my voice.

"Heyyyyy there." Tyler says as he slowly enters my room.

"Hey." I say quickly because I have no energy today.

He plops in my desk chair and says, "So I have something really good to put in the project."

"Ok, hit me with it." I say, getting a little excited that Tyler is actually taking this seriously.

"Ok. I think we should interview each other. We each write out 10 questions for each other. They can be social, educational, or relational. Each of us has to answer completely honestly and promise neither of us will judge each other based on our questions or answers. After we get our answers back, we will see how much B v. B has benefited us or not and what we need to do in order for it to benefit us and others." He says and just stares at me.

"Well, damnnnnn, Tyler!" I think to myself. After I collect my thoughts and say, "I think that's a dope idea. Let's get to work."

Maybe Whitney can bridge the gap between Tyler and me.

Interlude: Black Baby Jesus.

Dear Black Jesus - please make sure your boy Tyler doesn't get too real with his questions because I would hate to hurt his white boy's feelings. Amen, Ari. Oh, and whatever you're trying to teach me, please teach me how to do the single ladies dance properly without looking like Michelle. Sorry, Lord— I just thought I would throw that in there since you're already listening to a prayer or 2 from me.

Thanks again,

Your girl, Ariana.

Chapter 24

Kanye West (Post-Kardashian)

You know, I think everyone gives Kanye a hard time. He's just trying to bring everyone together and recognize that slavery is done, and people have to get out of that mentality. Now, I completely agree that African-Americans have been treated unfairly, and life has been hard. But why does everything have to be white people's fault? I have no issue with black people. My best friend Russell is black; he's like my brother from another mother.

Hi. I'm Tyler Manning, and like Kanye, I feel misunderstood, especially by Ariana. I'm trying really hard to get her to realize that I'm working just as hard on this project as her and that I'm just trying to figure out life just like her.

I come from a pretty well-known family. My dad is Chris Manning, a Democratic senator from CT. His father before him was a Senator, so my family is in the business of politics, and I guess it's assumed I will one day go into politics. My dad is a talented speaker with great ideas about what the perfect society would look like, and people say he has the "it" factor. The Obama meets Beto "it" factor. So, I guess his next political move will be a move to 1600 Pennsylvania Ave.

My mom, Kelsey Manning, is an amazingly smart woman. She's on the board of Planned Parenthood; she graduated magna cum laude from Wesleyan and went to Stanford Law, where she met my dad. She planned on becoming a professor of Law at Stanford, but love and the possibility of doing something great with my father took priority. So, she moved her life to the east coast, and now she collects American Art and sits on boards mainly dealing with women's rights.

I'm the spitting image of my father, and I have my mother's eyes. Tall, broad shoulders, sandy blonde hair, eyes as blue as the ocean, and a smile that could charm an old lady out of her walker. People say I have the "it" factor, but honestly, I want nothing to do with politics. I have no clue what I want to do or be when I grow up. Right now, soccer is all that matters to me. Oh, and doing well on this project because I don't think I can handle the wrath of Ari Whitaker.

Dear God- please don't let me ask the wrong questions because I don't want to offend Ari. Also, please let Bernie announce he's running for President—I think he could have totally beat the tangerine dude in the last election.

Chapter 25

Maya Angelou

"When someone shows you themselves the first time, believe them."

- Maya Angelou.

"Cai!" Malia yells as she tries to catch up to her in the hall. "Cai! I know you hear me!" she says as she catches up. Cai stops and looks at her with tears in her eyes. "Hey...what's wrong?" Malia says as she pulls her to the side.

"Nothing. Don't worry about it." Cai says while wiping her tears away.

"Cai. Come on, tell me. You haven't been acting yourself lately." Malia says.

"Listen, Lia. We can't do this anymore. I mean, this thing is just a phase, and it was fun while it lasted, right?" Cai says with no emotion.

"Wait. What?" Malia replies, feeling like she'd just been hit with a ton of bricks. "No. No, it's not. The first day we saw each other, you came up and introduced yourself, and I knew then that what I was feeling wasn't a phase. I knew these were feelings I had never had for anyone I have ever met." Malia says while trying to get Cai to look at her. "Cai, you're the sweetest, most genuine.

person I know, and I know that's who you really are. And I know you feel the same way I do."

"Listen, Lia, the first time I saw you, I thought that girl is the -Ish, she's smart and kind." She says like it's a distant memory. "But anyway, like I said, I can't do this. My parents found some of our notes, and they are pissed, to say the least, and say I need to focus on track because I'm going to miss out on my opportunity to get a scholarship messing around with you and this phase," Cai says, trying to hold back the tears. "So, it is what it is. We are always going to be friends." She hugs Malia and walks away. Malia stands in the hall feeling numb.

You know, everyone has associated Maya Angelou's quote, "When someone shows you themselves the first time, believe them." about a negative experience with people. But has anyone ever considered it was just meant to be an initial observation of an individual? Most people are good people, and our gut tells us who to love and trust, and most of the time, it's right. Let's hope Miss Angelou's quote means the glass is half full for Malia and Cai.

I walk into Miss Culver's room and see Malia sitting alone with her. I double-take and see her eyes are red. "Oh, sorry...I didn't mean to interrupt." I say, backing up toward the door.

"No. It's okay." Malia says as she wipes away a stray tear.

"How can I help you, Ariana?" Miss Culver asks.

"Ummm. Oh yeah, I was just stopping by to ask if you would help me with my speech for tomorrow's debate." I say, feeling totally out of place.

"Absolutely. Come back after school if that works for you." she replies.

"Great. I'll see you after school." I say and wave goodbye.

"Hey, Ari. Wait up!" Malia yells as she comes running up to me.

"Hey, girl. What's up?" I say, looking extra concerned.

"Cai broke up with me." She says, trying to hold back tears.

"What the what?" I say, surprised and upset for my best friend.

"Hey. After I'm done with Miss Culver, you should come over for dinner, and we can hang." I say as I give her a hug around the waist.

"Sounds good, just text me." She says as we split ways.

Chapter 26

Michelle Obama

"The only limit to the height of your achievements is the reach of your dreams and your willingness to work hard for them."

- Forever First Lady Michelle Obama.

The bell rings, and I walk into Miss Culver's room. "Hey, Mrs. Culver." I say as I stroll in, thinking about tomorrow's outfit for the debate. "Hello, Miss Whitaker. What can I help you with today?" She asks.

"Well, I just want to fine-tune some of my debate topics," I say as I sit down next to her. "You know I'm running against Kevin, and he's trying to give everything away for free, and that's just unrealistic, so I want to re-direct the topic to things like the Winter Social (aka a better playlist), after-school club funds and things like that," I say.

"Those sound like great ideas. Let's get to work." She smiles as she sits down next to me.

Did you know Michelle Obama hated speaking in public? She much preferred small groups of people so she could relate. Thank goodness President Obama brought her out of her shell because today, girls like me who are just running for school President have someone to aspire to be. After meeting with Miss Culver, I realized I should.

take Mrs. Obama's approach, and if Kevin goes low, I'll go high, and I'll keep my speech simple and inspiring instead of trying to one-up Kevin on every topic. If you speak to the people, they will speak back when it's time to vote. Thanks, Shelly O.

As I walk out of Miss Culver's room, I spot a photo of two people standing with Congressman Elijah Cummings, who also looks just like her, but they look black. Huh? I think to myself.

"Hey, Miss Culver, who are the people in the picture?" I ask.

"My parents," she says as she picks up the picture and hands it to me for a closer look. I grab the framed picture and do just that. Hold up...they are black, I think to myself, but obviously, my face also says it.

"Yes, Miss Whitaker, my parents are black." She says in her sweet voice with a sly smile.

"Okay...I see you, Miss C." I say with a big smile. I always knew Miss Culver was down for the cause.

Chapter 27

Beyoncé Part II

"From the top of the mornin', I shine."

— "I'M THAT GIRL."

You know, Beyoncé revolutionized the stages of relationships. She has been crazy in love, dangerously in love, she has been the best thing you never had, and drunk in love, to suddenly putting a bat in your windshield, and she wasn't sorry about it because you were not about to break her soul. And that, my friends, is why she is the Queen.

On my way home from school, I text Malia and tell her to meet me at my house at fifteen. As I walk up the driveway, I see Malia sitting there looking like a lost puppy. "Hey Lia. Why didn't you knock on the door? My parents are home."

"I dunno, just wanted some time to think, I guess." she replies.

"How was your meeting with Miss C?" Malia asks as she hops up.

"Really good. Girl, did you know Miss Culver was black?" I say, looking extra offended.

"You are cappin. Miss C has been pulling some reverse Rachel Dolezal stuff on us." Malia replies, feeling.

betrayed. "You know what, though—she always seemed like she had a little ratchet underneath that sweet voice of hers."

"Real talk, you're right. I guess she wasn't hiding it from us." I concede.

As I throw my stuff on the floor in my room, I ask Malia if she wants to listen to sad Beyoncé or Revenge Beyoncé. She decides to start with sad Beyoncé. "Alexa, please play the Sad Beyoncé mix," I say. "Now playing "If I Were a Boy" by Beyoncé," Alexa responds. Malia lays back on the bed and looks up at the ceiling while I try to think of an outfit to rock for the debate.

"Sooooo, do you wanna talk about it?" I say as I rummage through my closet. Where is my leather jacket?

"Ughhhhh," Malia rolls over, away from me, so I can't see her cry. "So, like I said. Cai decided to let me know I was just in a phase right before our six-month anniversary." she says and sits up, looking a little more angry than sad. "Alexa, play Beyoncé's Revenge mix." I demand quickly because I can tell the sad mix isn't doing it at the moment.

I sit down next to Malia and listen for a good 30 minutes about how it all unfolded and how it all ended today. She was in Miss Culver's room because Miss Culver saw how upset she was during class, so she pulled her aside and told her to come and talk to her if she needed to.

"Man, I don't even know what to do. I was going to ask her to the Winter Social. But I guess I'll be going solo again this year." She says, putting her chin in her hands, looking defeated.

"Yooo, you know you always have a date. Hello!!! I'm here and ready to slay all day!" I say, swinging my head back and forth, wishing I wouldn't have planned for a big Angela Davis for tomorrow.

"Thanks. I really appreciate it. Maybe I'll just skip it." she says as she shrugs her shoulders.

"Ohhhhhh H to the -L naw, you're not skipping the Winter Social! If I win, I'm in charge of the music!" I grab her by the shoulders and try to shake some sense into her.

"Oh yeah, I forgot. Well, we will see then." she says as she lays back down and requests that Alexa play the Sad Beyoncé mix again. I leave her alone and head back to my closet. I've decided the outfit must match the hair!

Chapter 28

Huey Newton

"I think what motivates people is not great hate but great love for other people"

- Huey Newton.

Huey Newton not only led a revolution for Black Americans during the civil rights era, but he also took it upon himself to make sure the youth of his community were fed and educated. You know, the breakfast and lunch program in schools was inspired by him and the women of the Black Panther Party. His Ph. D. in social philosophy helped black Americans to realize that they could no longer be silent and victims of oppression but needed to speak up through community outreach by forcing the oppressors out of power. His speeches were powerful and touched every corner of Black America.

Today, I woke up feeling extra excited and nervous. I put on my Beyoncé Girl Power Mix and hop in the shower. While I'm in the shower, I decide on the finishing touches of my outfit.

"Ari!" My mom calls up to me. "I made you breakfast."

"OK., Be down in a minute," I reply.

As I hit the last step, my mom looks up. Her eyes get wide, and a smile forms on her face. Black leather jacket, black turtleneck, brand new black jeans, and black leather boots. I'm channeling the "Sistahs of the movement." My fro is big and poppin (it better be I picked it out for 20 mins). I'm lookin like Angela Davis walked into Vogue and demanded Anna Wintour put her on the front cover.

"Ok, Ariana. Looking like Queen of the Young, Privileged, and Woke." She says while admiring the long pearl necklace I borrowed from her and paired with the outfit for contrast and class.

"Thanks, ma!" I say as I throw up my fist and sit down for breakfast.

As I walk into school, Russell comes walking up to me, "Wowwwww, Ari, you look...powerful." he says, looking mesmerized.

"Don't make her head any bigger, Russell." Malia Chimes in.

"Aht. aht. Don't hate, Lia," I say while throwing my hand up to stop the shade from trying to stop my shine. "Thanks, Russell," I say with a big smile. "Hey, did you get my text about putting up the extra signs?" I ask him.

"Yup. Yup. Nina dropped me off early, so they are all up."

"Awesome," I say, giving him a big hug. Is he wearing cologne?

"Ok. So, I'll see you guys at History and then the Auditorium for the debate." I say while doing my Serena victory twirl; I've been practicing. "Ok. See ya then." they both say.

"I hope your girl can fit her head through the doors," Malia says to Russell as they walk off.

"Ha. She will be fine. You know she gets like this when she's super nervous." Russell replies.

Malia sniffs. "Bro, are you wearing cologne?"

Russell's smooth, creamy skin blushes. "Uh...yeah, my mom got it for me, so I thought I would try it out today." He says, trying not to show his embarrassment while thinking he wishes Ari would have noticed.

"Hmm, oh ok. It smells good." She replies with a smile, knowing he wishes Ariana would have noticed instead as they walk into English class.

Chapter 29

Oprah Winfrey

Have you ever watched Oprah during interviews? She professes to be shy and kind of an introvert and says she rarely goes out. It's all so pure and genuine. But you put that woman in front of cameras with a mission, and she inspires the masses.

As we leave history class, Miss Culver wishes me luck, and I thank her for all of her help, throw up the Wakanda forever sign, and head toward the Auditorium.

"Ari, you look like a Queen." Erica compliments me as we walk into the completely full room.

"Thanks, girl." I say, trying not to show my nervousness.

"Remember Oprah said: "Think like a queen. A queen is not afraid to fail. Failure is another steppingstone to greatness, but you're going to do great. Keep your head up and speak your truth." she says as she hugs me.

"Damn, you're all philosophical today, E," I say, laughing off the nerves. "I just read it in the new O Magazine yesterday I thought it was meant to be." she replies.

I walk up to the stage and take a seat. I see the crew in the front row chatting. Russell looks extra nice today.

wearing his black J-crew sweater, dark blue jeans and his timberlands. Focus Ari!!!!

As the freshman finish their short debate and speeches, Principal Markowitz calls Kevin and me up to the podiums. As I walk, I try and channel my inner-Oprah, Michelle, and Shirley and put on a big smile as I look out into the audience. "Let's get this thing started." I say to myself.

"Good morning, Miss Whitaker and Mr. Martinez. You will each have 3 minutes for an opening speech, then students will have the opportunity to ask you a few questions, and then you will again have another 3 minutes for a closing speech." Principal Markowitz says, "Miss Whitaker, you may begin when you are ready."

"Hello, my fellow students of Ruth Bader Ginsburg Prep." I begin my speech, and the rest is a blur of 10th- grade history.

Chapter 30

'90s R&B

New Edition, Jodeci, 112, Boyz II Men. My mom's music that is still so relevant today. When your parents put it on, you can't help but think, where did that music go? Now, don't get me wrong, Cardi, Migos, Drake, and Khalid are still my jam, but something about the way that 90s R&B makes you feel is special.

After I walk off the stage, I feel like I'm floating. You should have seen it. Everyone is standing up and clapping. I put the bro, Kevin, in his place and made really great points about getting more school-funded functions and upping the budget for the Winter Social. It was great! Thank you, Oprah and Michelle, for your black girl magic.

"Ommmgeee, Ari! That ish was dope." Erica says as she meets me at the back of the auditorium.

"I told you you were going to SLAY, bestie." Malia says as she grabs me into a big hug.

I turn to Russell and say, "So what did you think, Mr. Campaign Manager." Russell stands there with this star- struck look, but there's something else there I can't quite put my finger on.

"Yoooooo, that was awesome, Ari," he finally gets out.

"How bout I treat everyone to some froyo." I say, super excited. I text my mom and ask her to order an Uber for us.

As we sit down with our overly filled froyo bowls, I finally exhale, "Y'all, that was the most amazing feeling up there. I was in the zone".

"Ari, I have never seen you so focused before." Malia says.

"It must be that outfit." Erica adds.

"Yeah, you looked fierce and it came out in that speech." Russell says.

After we all finish our froyo we say our goodbyes. Malia has basketball practice; Erica has to go help Eric with his biology homework so that leaves me and Russell standing there alone. "Hey, Nina will drop you off at home. I don't want you in an Uber alone." Russell says.

"Ok, cool, that would be great," I respond.

Nina pulls up and we jump in and tell her about the debate and speech. "That's great, Ari. I hope you win."

"Thanks," I say as I sit back. Nina then turns up her music. Today, she's rocking 90s R&B. Boyz II Men's song "On Bended knee" comes on, and all of us are singing away and bobbing our heads. Gosh, I love this music. We really missed out on the good stuff—I think to myself.

"Thanks for the ride, Nina." I say as I hop out of the car.

"Oh, I'll walk you to the door." Russell says as he hops out behind me.

"Ok..." I shrug.

We get to the door. "Well, thanks so much for helping me with my campaign. I couldn't have done it without you." I say, smiling at Russell.

"Oh, no biggie. I know you got this thing in the bag." he replies. As I turn to walk in the door, Russell mumbles, "Uh, hey, Ari."

"Yeah, what's up?" I reply. "Well. I was thinking maybe you might want to go to the winter social with me." he says while rubbing the back of his head without making eye contact. I double-take, and my infamous eyebrow raises, but thank god his head is down.

"Ummmmmm...Listen, Russell..."

"No biggie," he interrupts. "I just thought maybe..." "No. No." I interrupt him (this convo is not going very far). "Let me think about it. I have so much on my mind, and I haven't even started planning an outfit for the Winter Social." I lie (of course, it's planned).

"Oh, ok. Cool. Well, either way, we will both be there anyway—together." He says, his cheeks as red as the strawberries he had on his froyo.

"Alright, well, I better get going." he waves quickly and heads back to the car.

"Ok. See ya." I say as I walk into the house. I shut the door behind me and think. "WTH just happened," and he was definitely wearing cologne.

Oh, shoot! Tyler will be here in an hour. I have to finish up my questions. I think to myself as I run up to my room.

Chapter 31

W.E.B DuBois

"Education is that whole system of human training within and without the school house walls, which molds and develops people."

- W.E.B. Dubois.

Before BvB, W.E.B DuBois fought for educational equality. He was the founder of The Niagara Movement, a black civil rights organization founded in 1905, and its main purpose was a call for opposition to racial segregation and disenfranchisement. Therefore, BvB was the final nail in the coffin of desegregation. But was it?

"Present statistics show that predominantly white schools are more likely to enter into higher education than predominantly black schools," I started our project. "Why, you ask?" As I hold up a chart that Tyler and I put together. As we progress through our project, I look over at Tyler, and he is doing a great job; he doesn't look too bad either with his sandy blonde hair and striking blue eyes, dressed in his khakis and Brooks brothers button-up. He does an amazing job introducing our interview material and how we analyze our responses. After the interviews, we concluded that though we grew up with the same basic educational and financial backgrounds, our social experiences and expectations are vastly different. For instance, I didn't recognize that most of Tyler's.

ignorance about current events and current cultural novelties stemmed from his fear of asking. He was so afraid to ask a simple question, and he thought it was better left alone and it was easier to formulate his own opinion rather than asking the source for fear that it would be viewed as racist or offensive. Also, Tyler pointed out that he didn't realize his ignorance of such things further isolated his black schoolmates and friends, and therefore, there was a disconnect in their relationship, which hindered the true feeling of trust.

Once we finish our presentation, we both sit down and exhale. "Great job, Miss Whitaker and Mr. Manning," Miss Culver says approvingly. Tyler looks over with that charming smile, and I think, 'I guess I can tolerate him for a few more years.'

As I look over at Ariana, I realize how beautiful and smart she is. Her smile is just as brilliant as her brain. Where the heck have I been? I was a total idiot when I was 5.' Tyler thinks to himself as he watches Ariana talking to Russell. 'I gotta let her know I remember what happened and how sorry I am...'.

Chapter 32

Rihanna

"People think because we're young, we aren't complex, but that's not true. We deal with life and love and broken hearts in the same way a woman a few years older might"

-*Rihanna.*

"Hi, mami," I say to my mom as she puts together the last touches on a dish for a party.

"Hi, Erica. How was your day, baby?

"Great. I think I did really well on my presentation. We get our grades back next week." I say, trying to gauge her mental state.

"Awesome. That boy Derrick was very nice and seemed quite smart." my mom says as she moves around the large kitchen.

"Yeah, he's great!" I reply.

"The girls must be all over him. I'm sure he's dating a nice cheerleader or something." she says as she looks up at me.

I stand there with my mouth open. "Oh yeah. You know the girls love him." I say, trying to control my face.

"I bet. Hey, sweets, will you help me carry this out to the truck?" My mom asks.

"Sure thing." I say, knowing that this Derrick thing is going to be a lot more difficult than I think.

I wish I was more like Rihanna. She seems so free and outspoken. Sometimes, I imagine she's my older sister, and I ask her for advice on boys, make-up, fashion, and how in the heck she keeps that bangin' body while enjoying Caribbean cuisine. In my dreams, she tells me to just speak up and tell the entire world how I feel about him and to work out more. I ignore the latter because I just hate getting sweaty. Ugh!! Why can't my life be as easy as hers? She loves hard and out loud, and here I am, stuck inside this bubble of tradition. My parents are going to have to find out sooner or later because I love Derrick.

Chapter 33

Pam Grier

I am sitting on the floor while my mom is braiding my hair (I'm going for Alicia Keys circa 2001). My parents and I are watching old movies. Tonight's feature is Jackie Brown, played by the beautiful Pam Grier. Pam Grier was the Halle and the B(e)rry. Ya, dig. She was fierce, strong, and just an overall badass. She crossed the boundaries of color with her action-packed movies and style. I'm definitely feeling inspired and motivated for Election Day tomorrow.

I walk into the front doors of the school, rocking braids with wooden beads, a ripped-up pair of jeans, a striped crop top, a denim shirt tied around my waist, rust-colored timberlands, and big wooden earrings that look like the continent of Africa. I notice Russell and Tyler and shoot them a smile and a wave. I've been trying to figure out what to say to Russell since that awkward moment. I mean, he's my best friend, but something about him has changed, I mean, besides the facial hair and cologne. He's growing into his own, and it was a really big deal that he got up the courage to ask me to the Winter Social. Ughhhhh!!!! What am I going to do? Listen, I think to myself, I can't worry about that now. It's Election Day, and I feel like I'm on the Viewer's Choice red carpet, and.

I would have Zendaya feeling some type away by all of this greatness.

"Good morning, Ladies and Gentlemen. This is Principal Markowitz. This is your reminder to vote. Please remember that every vote counts, meaning the popular vote always wins. You have until 3 p.m. to cast your votes in the auditorium, where you will be required to sign off. Thank you for your attention, and Go RBG Prep Dissenters!" As Principal Markowitz gets off the loudspeaker, I see Tyler walking toward me.

"Hey there, Ari." he says as he leans against the wall next to my locker, which I need to clean immediately.

"Hey Tyler, what's up?" I ask, confused because Tyler never comes looking for me to have a conversation. "Nada just wanted to see if you finished your homework for Geometry..." he asks awkwardly.

"Uh, yeah..." I say, giving him a weird look. "Oh, ok, cool. Well, I'll see you in history." He says as he backs away and walks back toward Russell.

Meanwhile, across the way, Russell is watching the entire scene transpire as Erica and Eric talk to him. He has no clue what they are talking about because he can't believe what he's seeing. Is Tyler Manning crushing on Ari? He thinks to himself. No. He's just seeing things. He interrupts the twins and tells them he will text them after school and then walks off to figure out what in the world just happened.

"Hey, Bro, what was that about with Ari?" Russell asks Tyler as he walks back up. "Oh, nothing. Just asking if she finished her geometry homework," Tyler replies. "Okayyyy," Russell says with a confused look.

"Oh hey, do you know if Ari is going with anyone to the Winter Social?" he asks. Russell abruptly stops and looks at Tyler. "What's wrong, dude?" Tyler asks.

"Oh, nothing. I think I forgot something in my locker." Russell lies as he turns away to walk away from Tyler. "Oh. Ok. I guess I'll see you in class." Tyler says as he walks in the other direction.

Chapter 34

Are you Key, or are you Peele?

You know, some of the greatest comedic performances have been duos. Louis and Costello, Wilder and Pryor, Fred Sanford and Ester Anderson, and for our generation, Micheal Keegan Key and Jordan Peele. I mean, who hasn't seen the A-Aron skit without falling out? But like most duos, one member ends up excelling because they decide that the risk of going solo and going out on the proverbial limb is worth it. That's exactly what Jordan Peele did. He saw a moment and seized on it, and Get Out was a blockbuster hit that has put him on the top with cinematic greats. I mean, the man pulled Lupita N. for his film "Us," so sometimes you have to take the leap to get what you want.

As I walk into history, I see the crew is already there, so I go grab a seat next to Russell. "What's the T?" I ask everyone.

Erica immediately starts speaking a mile a minute, "Well, I tried to tell my mom about Derrick, but she chimes in and says he must have a cute cheerleader girlfriend and he's such a nice boy and… and… and…" she continues, but I'm lost, at one point she says Rihana gave her advice, but I guess the gist of the story was she still hasn't told her parents that she and Derrick are dating. My.

advice is maybe she needs more Sasha Fierce in her life than Rihanna. Note to self: Make Erica a Beyoncé "Sasha fierce" mix.

Malia shrugs her shoulders and says she's just been practicing and doing schoolwork. I immediately notice that Malia is in just a plain white V-neck tee, a pair of cut-offs, knee-length jean shorts, and a pair of chucks. Now, I know that seems stylish enough for some, but that sends up red flags that my bestie is taking this breakup with Cai pretty hard. Note to self: Make Cai a Beyoncé "love mix," so she sees how much she misses Malia, and keep Malia away from the Beyoncé "Revenge mix" until this thing is fixed.

I then turn to Russell, and he looks like he's in his feelings about something, "Hey Russell," I say with a big smile, "How was your weekend?".

"What's up, Ari." he says back. Is his voice getting deeper?

"Not much, just chilled and played soccer." He continues.

"Cool," I respond.

"Hey, my mom is making her famous Tuscan Salmon that you love. You wanna come over for dinner? It will be your victory dinner." he asks with his million-dollar smile. I blush a little (thank the ancestors for this ebony skin), but I have no clue why, so I respond, "Yeah, sure. That sounds like a great idea." I say as I turn around to face the front of the class.

Is it me, or is something in the air today? I think to myself. It must be the power of Pam Grier. I laugh to myself as Miss Culver starts class.

Chapter 35

Hillary Rodman Clinton

"Women are the largest untapped reservoir of talent in the world."

- Hillary Clinton.

I honestly try to forget election night of November 2016, and I only picture the feeling I had in the Summer of 2016 when Michelle Obama gave that amazing speech, and Hillary Clinton walked out on that stage to become the first woman to ever win a major party's nomination for the president of the United States of America. That moment should always give girls like me hope and inspire us to jump higher and reach farther.

"Good afternoon, ladies and gentlemen. This is Principal Markowitz. Polls have officially closed, and the votes will be counted and announced before the last bell of the day. Good luck to all of our candidates. May you realize the power of a vote and recognize this is just the beginning of your civil duties to society."

As Principal Markowitz goes off of the loudspeaker, I can feel my heart through my chest. My mind is at max capacity with thoughts. What if I don't win? But what if I do? I'm going to have to get started on the theme and playlist for the Winter Social immediately.

Tyler taps on my shoulder and interrupts my thoughts. "Hey, Ari," he says, trying to look cool.

"Hey, Tyler," I say. "You feeling alright?" I ask him

"Yeah. Why do you ask?" he responds.

"Oh, no reason. Just wondering. Anyway, what's up?" I ask, trying to change the subject.

"Well, I was wondering if you wanted to get together for froyo later to celebrate our project and your win?" I look around, wondering if Tyler is really asking me out to froyo...what in the world is happening here? "Oh, that sounds like so much fun, but I'm going to have to ask for a rain check because I'm actually going to Russell's for dinner tonight," I answer.

"Oh. Ok. Yeah. Cool. Maybe we can do it tomorrow then. No biggie." he says with a bit of disappointment in his voice.

"Yeah, that sounds good," I say. "Cool. See you tomorrow, and good luck. I know you got this in the bag." he says, winking that exquisitely blue eye.

"Thanks," I say with a goofy smile.

At that same moment, Malia walks up and looks at me, then at Tyler, and then back at me, and shakes her head. "What!? He just wanted to get together for froyo to celebrate the future president." I say, trying to sound innocent.

"Mhmmmmm," she responds. "What time are you going over to Russell's for your victory date?" she asks with a smirk on her face.

"Um...it's not a victory date," I say, again trying to sound innocent. We are simply celebrating our hard work on my campaign. This could have been you had you been a good friend and taken the position when I asked." I say, rebutting her date accusation.

"Mhmmmmm." she says again, side-eyeing me. "Anyway, text me when you get home from dinner. She says and walks away, trying to prevent Cai from walking toward us.

As I sit in the last period, the loudspeaker interrupts everyone's conversations. As Principal Markowitz announces the 9th-grade winners, I get this crazy feeling in my belly. "And we would also like to congratulate our 10th-grade candidates and the elected representatives for the Sophomore class for President, Ariana Whitaker."

I don't even hear the rest because I'm jumping up and down, screaming like I just won tickets backstage for the Renaissance tour! I hit my praise dance and turn around and hug the first person I see, who happens to be my partner in crime, Russell. He hugs me back, and we stay a minute too long, but it doesn't matter because this victory means everything. I then turn to Malia and Erica, who are "woot wooing" me and jumping up and down.

Then, as I do my Serena Victory twirl, I spy Tyler smiling at me and clapping.

Winter Social, here we come. The theme color will definitely be White for Girl Power!

Chapter 36

Naomi Osaka

"In a perfect dream, things would be set exactly the way you would want them. But I think it's more interesting that in real life, things aren't exactly the way you planned."

- Naomi Osaka.

I often think about how dynamic my parents are. My mother, Pat, is a very outspoken and passionate woman, and my father, Philip, is intense yet reserved. I guess people would say I'm like my mom on the court, but my daily demeanor is more like my father's.

There's this amazing tennis player that I love to watch because she reminds me of myself. Fierce on the court and shy in public. Her name is Naomi Osaka, and she just so happens to be black and Asian. I often see how hard it is for her to deal with the issue of being different. In every interview, she's always represented as the first Asian this or first Asian that, and every time, she politely corrects them that she is also, in fact, black. I always wonder how she deals with the daily expectations from her parents and coaches and the preconceived notions of fans and the media. I, like her, have the same issue but the opposite —everyone always describes me as black, forgetting that I have an entire family of Asian descent.

People also don't know how close my dad and I are. He's my rock, and I never want to disappoint him.

"Hey, MnM." my dad greets me when I walk in the door from school. It's super unusual for him to be home before I am, so needless to say, I'm surprised and excited.

"Hey, pops." I say as I walk over and give him a hug. He always gives the best hugs, and I definitely needed one today. We both sit down on the couch, "So, how's life? I feel like we are two-passing ships in the night lately." he says with a guilty look in those beautiful almond eyes.

I take a deep breath, and before I know it, tears start streaming down my face. "What's wrong, MnM? Did something happen at school? Are you and Ari fighting?" he asks while trying to grab me up into his arms. I can't say anything. This wasn't planned. I don't know what to do.

He gently lifts my face and wipes away my tears. "Malia, please tell me what's up." He pleads with me. "Dad...I..." I barely get out between sobs. I will myself to stop crying because I can't tell him what the real issue is. "Malia. You can tell me." He says, willing me to speak with his gentle eyes. "Listen," I say. "It's just been a really tough week with basketball and school," I lie. "I guess I just needed a good cry." I say, getting up to go to my room and continue the cry fest I've had for the past week.

"Ok, hunny." he says with a concerned look. "Well, if you need to talk, you know I'm here." He jumps up and kisses me on the forehead.

"Thanks, pops." I say as I walk upstairs.

As I shut the door, I slide to the floor and just cry. Is it about Cai? Is it about the world's expectations of me? Is it about disappointing my parents, especially my dad, because I'm gay? I don't know. But something has got to give because I can't do this anymore.

Chapter 37

Barry and Shelley

"Your story is what you have, what you will always have. It is something to own."

- Michele Obama.

When I get to Russell's house, they greet me like I've just won an Oscar. Ms. Audra made me my favorite dish, Ms. Sara got me a bouquet of calla lilies, and Nina made me chocolate cake. I really feel like Barry O. at that moment. No one expected me to win. Tyler Bros are a part of the popular kids, and the school is predominately white. I guess times are changing at RBG Prep, and hope lives on.

"You guys are way too sweet." I say as I stuff my face full of chocolate cake.

"We are just so proud of you," Ms. Audra says. "You should have seen how excited Russell was when he came home and told us."

"Well, thank you. And I totally couldn't have done this without my Russell," I say. Wait, did I just say my Russell?

"I mean, just Russell, he's yours, not mine." I try to rebound from my previous statement.

"We get what you're saying, Ari," Ms. Sara covers me.

I look over at Russell, and he hasn't really said a word since dinner. Not in a weird I'm not talking to you way, more like he's just observing, which is okay because he's nice to look at. Wait, what is going on? ALERT! ALERT! Do not pass-go. Do not collect $200. My brain is screaming. "Uh, I think I have to go," I abruptly say. "I need to get home and finish some last-minute stuff for school. I totally forgot," I say, trying to stuff the last piece of cake in my mouth. Russell looks at me, confused because he knows we have no homework, but he doesn't say anything.

"Okay, Ri-Ri, let me just grab my keys, and I'll take you home." Ms. Audra replies.

As she goes down to grab her keys, Russell hops up and says he will ride along. When we get in the car, I try to act normal. Ms. Audra turns on her car and listens to her news on satellite radio while Russell and I ride in silence in the back. My hand is tapping on the seat, hoping each tap gets me home quicker because I feel like I'm about to explode, and then I feel Russell's warm, soft hand cover mine. I look over at him, my eyes as big as the moon, and look away quickly. He keeps his hand there for a moment, and right before we pull into my driveway, he pulls it away.

"Well, thanks for the great night." I say as I rush out of the car.

"You're very welcome, and congrats, Ri-Ri." Ms. Audra says.

"Night, Ariana." Russell says.

"Night." I say and shut the door. As I walk away, I wonder if that's how Michelle felt when Barack first held her hand.

I have got to text Malia.

Chapter 38

LeBron James

"I always say, decisions I make, I live with them. There's always ways you can correct them or ways you can do them better. At the end of the day, I live with them."

- LeBron James.

We all sit down at the lunch table, chatting about the win and what songs we want to hear at the Winter Social. I can't help but think how normal this feels, but at the same time, every time I look at Russell, I get goosebumps. That was weird last night, right? But not weird in an eww way, but weird in a way that felt way too comfortable.

"Hey Ari, I have an extra ticket to the game tonight," Malia says. "And King James is off the injured list," she smiles.

"Yasssssss!" I say, trying not to scream. Everyone knows I love Bron Bron, not just for his amazing talent and beautiful, God-like body but also for his philanthropy, entrepreneurial mind, and commitment to his community and education. He's the real deal.

"OMG, what am I going to wear???" I say as I try to plan an outfit. Malia's parents got box seats for them, but they got Malia 2 tickets 3 rows up behind the team. So, you know I'll be trying to get an autograph. "Cool. So, we will pick you up at around 6:30-ish."

She actually means 7-ish because some stereotypes are true. "Awesome, I will be ready."

As I turn to look up at the clock, I see Tyler walking toward me. "Hey." he says as he sits on the edge of the table. Did I mention we sit on opposite sides of the lunch room, and Tyler has never walked over to this side?

"Hey," I say, and I can feel that all eyes are on me.

"So, are we still down for froyo after school? I knew you were going to win." he says with that Chris Hemsworth smile.

"Uh yeah, that should be fine." I say, trying to sound normal.

"Okay, cool. I'll order us an Uber, and I'll meet you outside after school," he says as he gets up and daps Russell. "Hey bro, you good?" he says to Russell.

"Uh yeah, I'm Gucci." Russell responds with a confused look on his face. "Cool, I'll see you at practice tonight then," Tyler Says.

"Cool." Russell replies.

"Sooooooo, what's that about?" Erica asks. "Nothing. He just wants to congratulate me on my win." I suck my teeth and try to regain control of the situation.

"Mhmmmmmm," she rolls her eyes. "Since when does Tyler come over here?" she asks. She has a point, you know—I think to myself.

"Listen, why are y'all always hatin' on this Diva? Just let me be great. People want a piece of the President now." I say jokingly.

Across the table, Malia is smirking, and Russell is simmering. Boy, oh Boy, this is like when Bron left Cleveland and went to Miami. Just let him be great!!!

The last bell rings, and I meet Tyler out front as requested. "Hey, hey." I say, smiling at him. Today, he is dressed like a vineyard vine model on his way to Martha's Vineyard, which is the exact opposite of me. Today, I'm wearing a shirt with all the greats on it, Michelle, Hillary, Rosa, and Maya, on top of Mt. Rushmore with a jean skirt and chucks.

"Hey, you." he says. Goodness, his eyes are bluer than blue today. "Shall we?" He says as he opens the Uber door for me.

"Thanks." I say as I slide into the Toyota Prius. Does every Uber driver drive a Prius?

Tyler pays for the froyo, and we sit down and chat for a while about nothing. "So, Ari...I just wanted to tell you something." he says, playing with the fruity pebbles on the top of his froyo.

"Okayyyy," I respond, scowling a bit. "So, you remember when we were doing the interview, and you.

mentioned you had a crush on someone when you were a kid, and they made you feel bad?" He says as he puts his spoon down. Ughhhh, is he really about to ruin this delicious moment?

"Yup, I remember." I reply. "Well, I know it was me you were talking about, and I just want to apologize and explain." he says.

"Tyler, seriously. You do not have to explain the decisions of a 5-year-old. It so ain't that deep, bro." I say because I'm annoyed at the fact that it still bothered me a little.

"Well, you're wrong about that whole thing. It didn't have anything to do with the fact that you were black. My friends were teasing me because they knew I liked you too, and I hated being teased, so I was dumb and said I didn't like black girls to get them off my back." he admits. "It was dumb and hurtful, and I wish I would have known back then how dumb it was." he says, looking sincere.

Wait, what in the world is going on right now? What did he say? I cannot process this right now. This was supposed to be a froyo and chill (not that chill) kind of day. I was really looking forward to this froyo, and now

Tyler is hitting me with some deep-seated kindergarten guilt.

I laugh a little because I have nothing better to do. "Tyler, wow," I say. "Um, thank you for admitting that. It really means a lot. That was super cool of you to say." I say, trying to process the entire conversation.

"Well, I just wanted to get it out in the open and let you know I see you, Ari," he says. Well damn, Tyler. I think. "You are amazing, smart, and funny, and you make me think about things other than myself and soccer." he says.

"Oh. Okay. That's nice." I respond, not knowing where this is coming from or where it's going.

"So I don't know if you're going with anyone to the Winter Social, but I just thought I would put it out there and ask if you want to go with me?" He says as he puts his head down and continues to eat his melting froyo.

Everything in me is screaming to get up from this table and run far away from here. This is not happening, but here I sit.

"Uh. Wow. I wasn't expecting that." I say, looking around, trying to remember where I'm at. Froyo shop in the center of town. Oh yes. Okay.

"Hey. Let me think about it, and I'll get back to you because you know I'm just now planning the winter social, and I just won the election. So let me get those things in order, and I'll get back to you," I say, trying to get my feet to move.

"Yeah. Sure. That's totally fair." he replies, not looking completely defeated.

"Cool," I say and eat my froyo in silence.

"Girlllllllll..." I say to Malia as I get into her mom's new Tesla.

"Hello, Ari." Ms. Pat interrupts me.

"Oh. I'm sorry. Hi, Mr. and Mrs. Wu." I respond politely. We all know Malia's mom is a stickler for manners.

"What's up?" Malia says to me, looking super excited to talk about something other than Cai.

"I'll tell you when we get to the seats," I say, trying to hold it all in. "Let's just say LeBron is devoted to Cleveland, but Miami is looking mighty fine" I say, trying to give her clues.

"Um, okay..." she responds, completely lost.

Chapter 39

Brandy and Monica

"Stay true to yourself because it goes a long way. If you don't know who you are, who are you really?"

- Brandy Norwood

There's this song that comes on when my mom feels like reminiscing about her childhood. And when she's really into it, she makes me sing a part of it. The song "The Boy is Mine" is a 90s black cult classic. The two girls like the same boy, and they are having a lyrical battle in falsetto. Anyway, no one ever knows who gets the boy, but let me tell you, that song is hitting close to home at the moment.

"Ok, what in the heck is going on?" Malia says as we sit down in our fabulous seats.

"Wait, how did you end up with an extra ticket?" I ask.

"This was the game I was going to bring Cai to for our 6-month anniversary." she says, looking sad.

"Damn, I'm sorry for asking, Lia," I say, putting my hand on her arm. "Let's just have a good time and take lots of selfies for Snapchat and the 'gram," I say, pulling out my phone. Tonight, we are twinsies, both rocking our Lebron Jerseys.

"Say, King James." I say as we smile for our first of many selfies.

"Girllllll...." I begin again and give her the tea on Russell and Tyler.

"So, you're telling me that Russell and Tyler have both asked you to the Winter Social, and you have hurt both their feelings by putting them off." Malia says, looking at me like I'm crazy.

"I have not hurt their feelings." I say, defending myself, "They are just both on a brief hold. What am I going to do?" I say in a slight panic. "Russell is my best friend, but Russell is getting fine," I say in my Wendy Williams voice. "But Tyler has changed, and it's damn hard to say no to the baby blues." I continue, feeling torn.

"Well, I guess you're in a conundrum, and Beyoncé doesn't have a song to get you out of this situation," she says, grinning like a crazy woman. "Lia. You know what? You're not helping. And I'm sure Beyoncé has a song. I just have to find it." Please, Queen Bey, have a song—I pray—I need to figure this out like yesterday.

We continue watching the game and cheer like mad women, and I do end up getting Lebron's autograph.

Chapter 40

Ava DuVernay

"If your dream is only about you, it's too small."

- Ava DuVernay

Miss DuVernay has created some of the most provocative and enlightening stories for African Americans. She is one of the leading directors and producers in the public eye today. What she has been able to do with the black experience is eye-opening and inspiring.

I'm watching Queen Sugar and crushing on Kofi. Is he not the finest piece of chocolate you have ever seen? (If you disagree, then you need glasses). A text pops up from Cai, "Hey, can you talk?" I read.

I text back, "Sure. Call you in 5." Lawddddd, I must love Malia to interrupt my weekly binge-watching of Kofi.

I run upstairs and get my thoughts together. "Ok. Work your magic." I say to myself as I dial up Cai.

"Hey." she answers, sounding like she's hiding in a closet.

"Hey." I whisper. Wait, why am I whispering? I'm not in a closet.

"How are you?" I speak up.

At first, there's silence, but she finally answers, "Honestly, I'm miserable, girl. I can't think straight." "I'm sorry." I say.

"Ari, I need your help. I really messed up, and Lia just avoids me," she says, sounding like she's trying not to cry.

"She's my best friend," she says (well, actually, heffa, she's mine—but I'm not in the business of being petty today).

"I know," I say. "Listen, Cai, Lia is hurting bad. She almost came out to her dad the other night..." I continue.

"Wait. What? She was going to tell her dad? She's so afraid that she will disappoint him if he ever finds out." she says with disbelief.

"Exactly," I reply. "Listen, y'all are young, and maybe it won't be a forever thing, but you guys found each other for a reason, and it was to support each other through this, right?"

"Yeah. You're right. I just feel like such a dummy now. I really care about Lia—I mean, I love her, and I never want to hurt her. But I did, so I don't know what to do to try and convince her I WANT her back, and I don't care who knows because you only live once," she says.

"Mhmmm. I get it. This is a story Ava would want to write about. Young, black love..." I think maybe I'll write Ava and see if she will pick it up. Dreams require actions, people!

"Listen, girl, I have an idea, but you gotta be on board, and I choose the playlist..." I say before I hang up and start devising a plan to help Cai. "Operation Get Lia Back" is in full effect.

Chapter 41

Aaliyah

"I stay true to myself and my style, and I am always pushing myself to be aware of that and be original."

-Aaliyah.

Well, I know I said the theme for the Winter Social was going to be "white inspired," but I changed my mind because last night, I laid in bed and did homework listening to Aaliyah and thought she was such an original. She was young, strong, and kind and paved her way despite the trauma and abuse she had experienced. So, thinking like a queen, instead of being basic, I decided on a black theme instead of my original idea of Winter White. "Midnight in Paris" will be beautiful with bright stars everywhere, the Eiffel Tower will sparkle in the background, and a huge full moon will give the auditorium just the right mood. Good thing, dad is officially home until the end of the semester so he can turn my dream into reality. I've also recruited Erica's parents to cater the event and Wu, Black, Summers, and King to sponsor it. Listen, y'all, we have to support each other when we can.

This night is going to be a blast! All ticket proceeds will go to the Innocence Project.

"Hey guys." I say to the crew as I walk into history.

"Sooooooo, who wants to volunteer to be a part of the.

Winter Social Set-up Crew?" I say while holding a sign-up sheet.

"I'm in, Madam President." Russell says and gives me a wink and a chill goes through my body because I like the sound of Madam President, of course.

"I'm in charge of the stars." Erica says while she turns around, flirting with Derrick.

Malia just gives me a nod—So I assume she's in. Good thing they all said yes because I already signed them up.

"Awesome!" I say, feeling extra excited.

"Hey! You can count me in," Tyler says from behind me.

"Oh, okay. Cool. Thanks, Tyler." I say happily, surprised.

I look over at Malia, and she puts her head down and chuckles. I roll my eyes and sit down.

"Today, we are going to talk about Abraham Lincoln and the Emancipation Proclamation..." Ms. Culver says to begin class. At least I can get lost in history class and not have to worry about my Winter Social dilemma. But at the same exact moment, I'm about to raise my hand to point out a few facts that Miss Culver missed. I'm literally hit with a note. I open it and read it.

"Hey. I wanna be on the set-up team, and let's meet and discuss the plan —xo Cai!".

I look back, give her a look, and turn back around to re-focus, but I can't. Why is there so much drama coming at me all of a sudden? I just want world peace, a.k.a. a millennial uprising. I write back, "Uh, why are we passing notes like it's 1999? And okay, I'll put your name on the list. You know Malia is going to freak out on me when she sees you show up. Meet me at my house after school." I pass the note back and turn around to the front of the class, grinning like the Grinch who stole Christmas. Those two are getting back together because Sad-Malia is not fun to be around, and anyway, it's another thing to distract me from Russell and Tyler, who both look really good today in their soccer uniform tops, jeans, and team Nike Vapor Maxes customized in the school colors. They both look like they have fresh cuts, gelled and styled perfectly. And Russell is wearing his Tom Ford glasses today that make him look super smart.

"Miss Whitaker? Did you have something to say?"

Miss Culver interrupts my thoughts.

"Huh?" I respond, shaking myself back to reality.

"Your hand was up. So would you like to contribute to the discussion?" She asks me, looking amused.

"Oh. Yes, did you also know?" I go on about Abe, and for a few minutes, I forget about my own teenage drama.

Chapter 42

Bonnie and Clyde (The Bey & Jay Version)

"When you're truly in love. You will never have anything to hide."

Jay-Z

"Hey, Babe!" Derrick says as he walks up to the lunch table and sits down next to Erica.

"Hey." she says back, pushing her food back and forth on her plate.

"What's wrong?" He asks as he kisses her on the forehead.

"Nothing," she says as she sighs.

Me being me, I chime in, "Erica, just tell him your parents think he's dating some cute cheerleader, and therefore, you still haven't mentioned he's your date for the Winter Social."

Erica looks at me with her mouth wide open and then looks at Derrick and frowns. "Yeah, what she said."

"Babe, why don't you just let me come over and ask them if I can take you to the dance," he says. Everyone needs a Derrick. He's so polite and cute, too.

"I just don't know if that will work, Derrick. My parents are so overprotective." she says as she shoves her lunch to the side and puts her head in her hands. "Ughh, why can't we be like Jay and Bey and just do what we want?" she says. I see the Beyoncé mix I made her is giving her some inspiration.

"Babe. I'll always be your Clyde. You just say the word, and I'll be there." He says while lifting her head and sneaking a kiss before any teachers see. Now, I know I said they were cute, but eww-they are corny sometimes. But hey, even corny people need love.

"Thank you for always making me feel better. I'll figure something out before the dance. You just be ready to go when I give you the go-ahead." She says as she grabs his hand to go.

"You got it, Bonnie." he says as he follows her out.

"Those two are so." I begin to say, "Corny." Russell chimes in.

"Yeah, you're right," I agree.

"But doesn't everyone want that kind of love? That 90s teenage Romcom love." I say, smiling.

"Yeah. I guess." he replies with a smile on his face.

"Yeah, I guess." Malia replies not so excited.

"Lia. Have you heard from Cai?" I ask, already knowing that Cai has been texting her daily.

"Yeah. But like Bey said..." She starts to quote the Bey Revenge mix I made for her, but I interrupt.

"Remember that even when Bey is mad at Jay, she always gives him a chance to make it up."

"Let's not forget 4:44 was his apology to her, and they have been going strong like 2002 Bey and Jay," I say, trying to pull her out of her funk.

"Maybe you should listen to some Ella Mai to cheer you up." I suggest.

Yes—it pains me to turn on my girl Beyoncé, but desperate times call for desperate measures. And anyway, Bey and Jay have people out here breaking up while they are sitting in Paris sipping on Champagne...so yeah.

"Yeah. Maybe you're right." she says as she looks over at Cai.

Step 1 of Operation get Malia back is complete.

Chapter 43

Awkward Black Girl

"I thrive on obstacles. If I'm told that it can't be done, then I push harder."

- Issa Rae.

<u>Ari</u>

Now, I don't try to represent that I'm a part of the cool crowd. I don't hang out with Michaela Stone, and I certainly don't hang out with the Tyler Bros., and it's not because I don't like them. We all chat when we are in the same room or see each other out. But they are the kids from the movies. I'm just an awkward black girl trying to navigate this teenage journey. I'm lucky that I have a crew that gets it with me because there are a lot of kids out here trying to figure their lives out, and having my crew keeps me sane.

"Hey, Cai." I say as I walk up to my house. She's waiting outside, looking like she's already won a gold medal at the Olympics. Her body is perfection, but she never believes it when you tell her. She doesn't think she trains hard enough or eats well enough, and the list goes on and on. Being a teenager is hard. I wish there was a realistic book out there showing girls that every shape and size of a girl is perfection and that our bodies change and grow. Beyoncé said something to the effect that she loved.

having the extra weight on her after the twins because she felt "real and free." She felt womanly. I wish Cai wasn't so uncomfortable in her own beautiful skin. But I digress.

"Hey, Ari." she says, fidgeting with her jacket zipper.

"So, I spoke to Lia today and..." I tell her about lunch as we walk into the house.

Malia

"Malia Elaine," my mom calls up to me when she walks in the door.

"Hey, ma!" I say as I run down the stairs.

"Hi, sweetie. I came home early to see if you wanted to go shopping for the Winter Social." she says with a smile on her face.

"Oh, sure." I say as I try to fake a smile.

"OK, go grab your shoes, and we will leave in a few. I can't wait to pick a dress." she says as she walks off.

Have I mentioned I hate dresses? I just don't like the way I feel in them—I mean for church or some super special political event, sure. But this is a school dance and a dance I'm not sure I want to even go to.

As we drive to the mall, I'm dreading the dress my mom is going to choose. Don't get me wrong, my mom has excellent taste in fashion, and she's pretty cool about my wardrobe choices, but I know she wants to put me in some dress she's seen on the runway. I would prefer a.

sleek, fitted black pantsuit with a pair of custom Retro 9s (a girl can dream). But I'll end up with a dress and a pair of heels I can barely walk in.

"So, how is school?" She asks while we listen to Mary J. Blige.

"It's going." I say while looking out of the window.

"Well, that doesn't sound exciting." she says, looking over.

"What's up with my girl?" She asks as she puts her hand on my arm.

Gosh, I just want to scream it out to her, but I just can't.

"Nothing. Just nothing really interesting going on right now." I reply as I look out of the window at the buildings as we drive down the highway.

There is nothing worse than feeling like an awkward black girl...

Erica

"Erica Leigh!" my dad calls over to me while I'm studying at one of the back tables.

"Yes, papa!" I call back.

"Your mom said you needed money for a dress for the Winter Social." he says.

"Yeah, that would be great!" I respond, trying to get up the nerve to tell him I'm going with Derrick.

"Great. I'll give you money for you and your brother. Should I order a driver for you two?" he says as he hands me his credit card.

"Ummmmmm... OK." I say, trying to hide the horrified look on my face.

"OK. I'll get that ordered. You and your brother have a good time spending all of my money." he laughs.

I turn and look at Eric, who's also studying. He rolls his eyes at me because I'm too much of a coward to tell my parents I have a boyfriend. So, I roll my eyes back and tell him to get his stuff so we can leave.

I text Derrick, "It's go time. Tomorrow at the restaurant at 6:30."

"Okey Dokey" he texts back. I put my phone away. I know the exact dress I want, and it's going to be fiyah.

Chapter 44

Guess Who's Coming to Dinner

"Love takes off masks that we fear we cannot live without and know we cannot live within."

-James Baldwin.

'Guess Who's Coming to Dinner' is a movie about a black man dating a white woman, and she brings him home for the first time, starring the magnificent Sidney Poitier. Now, that doesn't sound incredibly dramatic, but this story takes place in the 60s when interracial couples were taboo. So, it was one of the first films to cross color lines. A remake starring Bernie Mac (Rest in Power), Zoe Saldana, and Ashton Kutcher takes the humorous route of pointing out that every generation deals with the issue of interracial dating, including mine.

"Ari!!! I need your advice." Erica texts me.

"What's up, girl?" I respond.

"Meet me at the mall in an hour." she says.

"Uh, OK." I respond back. "Daddy," I yell (he's an easier target).

"Sup, boo thang?" He answers back. "Will you take Cai and me to the mall? We need to go shopping for the.

Winter Social?" I say in the sweetest daddy's-girl voice I can conjure up.

"OK. Give me 15 minutes. I'm trying to get the base of your Eiffel Tower finished." he says.

"No prob," I say.

"Girl, we gotta get you a dress that screams take me back." I say to Cai.

"Ugh, I hate going clothes shopping." Cai responds, looking at herself in the mirror.

"Listen, Cai. I promise to make you feel like a million bucks once we are done shopping." I say, smiling at her.

"OK. If you say so...," she says hesitantly.

"Thanks, Daddy." I say as we hop out of the car.

"See you in 2 hours right here, Ari." he says, knowing that the mall is my Achilles' heel and an empty bank account is his.

"Yes, Dad. I promise. 2 hours max." I hold up my Girl Scouts honor sign.

We walk straight to the food court and meet Erica, who looks completely freaked out. "Hey, chica." I say as we walk up.

"Hey..." she says, looking confused when she sees Cai with me. The crew is "ride or die" for each other, so she's.

probably thinking Cai is the enemy right now. I look at her, knowing what she's thinking.

"Listen, I have a lot of balls in the air, and she's one of them, so stop throwing shade. I promise I'll explain later." I say, trying to diffuse the situation.

"OK then, Hey Cai." she says, still giving her the side-eye.

"Hey Erica." Cai replies, trying not to make any sudden moves.

"OK, so what is up for real, for real?" I ask Erica.

"OK, my dad sent Eric and me to the mall to shop for our outfits for the Winter Social, and my dad proceeds to say he's going to order a car for me and Eric to show up in... TOGETHER." she says, looking completely horrified.

"Damnnn, girl. That won't be cute." I say, not helping the situation.

"Duh. So, I texted Derrick and told him tomorrow is go time. We have got to tell them." she says, sounding completely panicked. Is it not 2023? Are we not living in a post-Ebony and Ivory world? Did Loving v. Virginia not teach us anything? Who am I kidding? Caribbean parents are stuck in their traditions, so we have to come up with a game plan." she says, sounding defeated.

"OK. It sounds like we have to make a serious plan, but first, we must shop because I've had this outfit planned in my mind since the day I said I was running for.

class President. So let's do some retail therapy and figure it out." I say as I lead them toward Nordstrom.

Meanwhile, on the other side of town, Derrick, Russell, and Tyler are all being fitted for their suits.

"Bro, I don't know how I'm going to pull this off with Erica's parents." Derrick says while he tries not to get stuck with pins.

"Dude, you are ballsy. I've known Erica's parents since I was a baby, and I'm telling you, this could either go wide left, or they will cook you a feast." Russell says as he looks at bow tie colors, trying to guess what color Ari is going to wear.

"I think it's very cool that you're putting yourself out there for your girl." Tyler chimes in as he picks up a pink tie, thinking that maybe Ari will be wearing her favorite color, pink, to the Winter Social.

"So, have either of you decided who you're going to ask?" Derrick winces as he gets stuck by a pin.

"Uh, still thinking. You know sometimes it better to go solo-dolo." Russell says as he finds the perfect color bow tie.

"Yeah. Me too. You know there are lots of fish in the sea." Tyler says as he checks his phone to see if Ari answered his text.

"Well, you guys better hurry up before you end up being each other's dates." Derrick says as he turns around, showing off his suit. Tyler and Russell both nod and laugh nervously.

"Okayyyy, Erica, I see you rocking that teal dress.

Looking like a Caribbean Queen," I say.

"You should totally get that dress. It fits every one of your gorgeous curves." Cai adds.

"Ha. Cai, you're kidding me, right? I'm trying to get like you with that figure." Erica laughs, admiring Cai's slim body in a beautiful pink dress that shows just enough tummy.

"Well, I think you both are going to kill it at the Winter Social." I say as I walk out of the dressing room in the outfit I have pictured in my head for the last 3 months.

"Dayummmmmmm, Ari!" they both yell out and run over to me.

"Beyoncé would be proud." Erica says.

"Thanks, boo!" I say as I look at my phone, seeing a text from Tyler asking me what color I'm going to wear. I ignore it. A true Diva never reveals her wardrobe choices.

"Oh crap!" I say, "We have to go; my dad will be out front in 10 minutes." All of us rush back into our dressing rooms, change, and pay for our clothes.

"Good luck, E. See you tomorrow!" I say.

"Thanks, guys, and good luck Cai!" Erica says.

"Thank you, guys, so much. I hope this plan works!" Cai says as she waves goodbye.

The next day flies by, and we all chat about our shopping experiences and how excited we are about the Winter Social. Malia's didn't go as well as everyone else's, but she says she was going to get her dad to go with her because she knew he wouldn't care what she got.

I overhear Tyler saying he went with pink because it compliments his eyes. Mhmmmm...and Russell says he found the color that he had been looking for but wasn't giving it away. The boys today are so fashion-forward. I love it.

After discussing the Winter Social, we all get down to business on how Erica and Derrick need to handle this meeting of the parents. Let's hope they take our advice.

Chapter 45

Dangerously in Love vs. Crazy in Love

"When opportunity presents itself, grab it.

Hold on tight and don't let go"

-Celia Cruz.

I'm sitting at the back table pretending to study.

"Dude. You're making me nervous," Eric says as he looks up from an empty sheet of paper.

"I know. I know." I say, trying to pull myself together.

I hear the front door open, and my heart nearly jumps out of my chest. "Welcome to Caribbean Paradise," I hear my mom say. "Oh, hi. Derrick. So nice to see you again."

"Hi. Mrs. Channing," he says in that sweet southern accent. This is my cue—I jump up and hurry toward Derrick. "Hey, Derrick. How are you?" I say, trying to act surprised that he's here.

"Hey Erica," he says, giving me a confident smile. He walks toward me and gives me a hug—I stiffen up a little but immediately fall into him and smell the fabric softener in his shirt.

"Well, what can we get you, sir? Come sit down.

Erica, go get him a menu," my mom says.

I walk and get a menu. Breathe, Erica 10...9...8.

"Hey, Eazy-E." my dad says to me as he walks out of the back office.

"Hey, Papa." I say, giving him a quick smile. "Oh, hey there, young man!" He smiles and waves at Derrick.

"Hi, Mr. Channing." he waves back as he takes a seat.

I hand him a menu and sit down with him. We both smile at each other, and he mouths— "It's ok." to me, and then says, "Hey, Mr. and Mrs. Channing..." I cut him off. "He just wants a coke, mom."

"Ok. No problem." my mom responds.

"Ok. I'm going to walk away and come back because I'm going to explode. You get my mom in a nice convo, and I'll be back." I say to him, "Ok. Bonnie," he winks at me. God, I love this boy.

As I walk away, I see my mom walk back up to Derrick. He starts putting that southern charm on her, and I see her smiling and fluttering those eyelashes. Perfect. I look at Eric and say, "It's go time."

"Godspeed." he responds and lifts his book up to cover his face.

As I walk back over, I see my dad bringing Derrick an appetizer. Ok. That's a good sign when my parents are feeding you, that means they like you.

"How's it going?" I say.

"Oh great. Derrick was just telling us about how excited he is about the Winter Social, and he can't wait for the food." My mom smiles as she looks back up to him. Man, he's good.

"Umm, Mr. and Mrs. Channing..." he clears his throat. "So, like I was saying. I'm super excited. But I also wanted to..." The door opens, and he's interrupted.

"Oh, excuse me, Derrick," my mom says as she greets the next customer. Darn it. That was the perfect moment. Derrick looks over at me, showing a little more distress than when he first walked in. I sit down with him and say, "We don't have to do this. I can just meet you at the dance."

"Absolutely not." he says to me in the most serious voice I've heard him use.

"Ok. But this is going to be more of a Romeo Must Die than a Romeo and Juliet thing if we don't hurry up and get it done." I say, exasperated, as I bury my face in my hands.

Derrick gets up and goes over to the bar area where my mom and dad are standing. I can't hear the conversation, but I can see the faces. Mom looks surprised and confused, and dad looks... Hmmmm... I don't know.

that face, but he doesn't look like he's about to throw Derrick out, so that's a good sign. They each smile at Derrick and signal for me to come over.

"Well, Erica. It looks like Derrick wants to ask you something." my mom says as she eyes both of us. So, Derrick turns to me as if he's about to get down on one knee and says, "Erica, will you go to the Winter Social with me?" My smile must have blinded everyone at that moment because I have never been happier.

"Yes," I say. "Yes." I say again as I giggle like a little girl with tears in my eyes.

"Uh, baby girl, he's just asking you to the dance," my dad says, patting Derrick on the back.

I laugh. "I know. I know. I just get emotional." I say as I give Derrick a huge hug.

"Well, sit down, Derrick. Today is your lucky day.

You get to be our taste tester." my dad says.

"Yes, sir." Derrick responds, eager to taste paradise.

After Derrick is stuffed with enough food to feed the entire sophomore class, he Thanks my parents and says goodbye. I walk him out around the corner, where he's waiting for his mom to pick him up, and I give him the best kiss he's never had. "Thank you so much, baby." I say, hugging him tight.

"No biggie! I think all is well. Russell warned me it was either going to go very wrong, or they were going to fix me a feast." He smiles.

As he pulls away, I walk back into the restaurant, and my mom calls me to the back office. As I walk in and shut the door, she smiles and says, "So how long have you and your little friend had that planned?" Giving me that all- knowing mother's look. I laugh nervously and sit down and spill my entire heart. She gets up and hugs me and says, "Well, my love, I think you got yourself a good one."

"But good luck telling your father. You know he thinks you're not supposed to like boys until you're 25." she laughs.

"Ugh. I know. I'll save it for after the dance," I say. I would hate for my dad to greet Derrick at the door with his butcher knife the night of the Winter Social, I think to myself. "Thanks, mami." I say, hugging her tight. Sometimes, Ari is right; you need a little Sasha Fierce and a Clyde to get it done.

Chapter 46

Halle x Chloe

"Don't try to lessen yourself for the world; let the world catch up to you."

- Beyonce.

Halle x Chloe were discovered by the one and only Queen Bey. One has a voice like an Angel, and the other has a voice straight from Mahalia Jackson, and when they come together, it just works. Malia is the Halle to my Chloe, or maybe the other way around.

Malia grabs me after lunch and says, "If you want to be my stylist, then here's your chance." "My dad is picking us up after the Winter Social meeting and taking me shopping."

"Yassssss, girl." I snap my fingers and back up, imagining what I'm going to dress my bestie up in.

"This is going to be phe-nom-e-nal." I say, grabbing her by the arm and blabbering about the color she should wear. Of course, I have the perfect color since couples should attempt to coordinate for events, in my opinion.

After school, Malia's dad picks us up and takes us to the mall. "Do you girls want me to go in with you?" he asks.

"Uhhhhh, no, Mr. Wu, we got this." I say while pulling Malia out of the car.

"Ok." he says, sounding relieved.

Malia and I walk into Nordstrom, and I tell her to sit down and let me get things put into the fitting room. I'm like a mad woman dashing all over the store, feeling like Anna Wintour just sent me out to dress Serena or Lupita for a cover. I get what I want in the fitting room, grab Malia, shove her in, and take a seat. This is going to be good. I know exactly what my best friend likes and needs to feel confident. She's going to look so great, I scream inside of my head.

We go through about 3 or 4 different outfits, and then she walks out looking nervous and happy. "O.M.G," I say. "That's it. That's the one." I smile and turn her around. She smiles, hits me with a little floss action, and walks back into the fitting room. Now it's time to find the perfect slippers for my Cinderella.

Mr. Wu picks us up with "Atomic Dog" blasting from the speakers. Did Malia never mention he and my father pledged Omega Psi Phi together in college? And that's why it's so embarrassing on Alumni Weekends. He turns down the music and says, "Hey, did you find what you wanted?"

"Yup," Malia replies with a huge smile on her face.

He looks back with that same smile and the same eyes.

"Good, anything for my girl." he says as he drives off and turns the music back up.

Bow, wow, wow yippee yo yippee yay....my best friend and I are about to shut the Winter Social down when we walk in.

Chapter 47

I'm Feeling Good

*"I'll tell you what freedom is to me: no fear.
I mean, really, no fear!"*

- Nina Simone.

Instead of my usual Beyoncé mix, I woke up to Nina Simone's "I'm Feeling Good." Bey should definitely think about doing a remake of this. I'm dancing around my room, getting ready for the last day of setup. My dad is packing his tools so he can finish the Eiffel Tower installation, and his crew is helping with the lighting and hanging the moon that Erica, Derrick, and Russell created. I have Tyler and Cai doing the table decorations, and Malia is helping me finish up the final touches and the playlist. I have all of the other volunteers hanging things and getting the selfie photo booth area ready. This dance is going to be EVER-Y-THING. And I have a huge surprise for the end—that I'm actually surprised Principal Markowitz approved.

"Ari, are you ready?" my dad yells upstairs.

"Just a minute." I say as I slip on my The Future is Female tee-shirt, throw my hair up in a big puff, and tie an African print head scarf around my edges (Gotta keep the edges laid).

I run downstairs, throw on some shoes, and kiss my mom bye.

"Have a good day, you two." she says as she grabs her coffee and disappears into her study. I don't think she does much studying there, and I hear "Kiss" sneak through the door.

"Okay, Daddy. I'm ready." I say and open the door for him so he can carry out his box of tools. As we drive, I think about the semester. So many ups and some downs, but mostly ups. Malia is the leading scorer and leading rebounder; Erica doesn't have to hide Derrick all of the time. Well, at least in front of her mom. Russell and Tyler were co-MVPs, and I'm just over here living my best life, no drama, doing well in school, and, of course, class president. But there is a little nagging feeling I have, but it will go away soon enough because the show must go on.

As we meet in the auditorium, everyone is super excited about the Winter Social. I'm on cloud nine because everything is going perfectly. My dad and his crew get the final touches of the installment together and check the lighting. If you could see it, you would think you were actually there. It is absolutely what I pictured in my head.

"Awesome job, Mr. Whitaker." Tyler says, admiring the work.

"Yeah. You ate that, Uncle Cal." Malia chimes in. Now, like I said, my father is a world-renowned artist, and his art is hung all over the world. But I don't think I've.

ever seen a bigger smile on his face than the one he is beaming us with right now. I couldn't be prouder either.

Russell comes up beside me and nudges me, "So, are you ready for tomorrow?"

"Beyond ready." I say, looking up at his handsome, Klay Thompson-looking face. Did he grow again?

"Cool. So, we will just meet here then."

"Yeah. My mom is going to drop Malia and me off a little early." I respond.

"Okay. Well, I'm going to get out of here. I gotta go hit my barber, Alex, up before he gets too busy. You know how they get, and I can't sit there and wait, listening to Soca all day."

"I feel ya." I laugh. "My hair appointment is at like 8 a.m. tomorrow, so I'll be pushing it." I say. You think I'm joking, but I'm not.

Erica and Derrick walk up, looking all in lust, and say goodbye. Then Cai comes up to say goodbye, smiling from ear to ear, and says that Malia actually spoke to her. Thank God! And last but not least, Tyler walks up, looking all sly mixed with Zac Efron, and says, "You sure you don't want me to pick you and Malia up? My dad got me a sick ride to show up in."

"Nah. We're good. I have stuff to get done, but I'll definitely see you tomorrow. And thank you so much for helping." I respond, trying to sound nonchalant.

"Okay. Then I will see you tomorrow. Promise you're going to save a dance or 2 for me." He says as he walks off". Goodness, he's good-looking, I think to myself.

When I say goodbye and thank all of the volunteers, my dad comes up to me and puts his hands on my shoulders. "Good job, boo thang." he says and kisses the top of my head.

"Thanks, Daddy." I say as we both admire our mini- masterpiece.

Chapter 48

Midnight in Paris

"Sometimes, what you're looking for is already there."

- Aretha Franklin

<u>7:15 a.m.</u>

When I think of midnight in Paris, I'm not thinking about that weird guy's movie. I'm thinking about the most romantic moment of the night, in Paris. When the clock strikes Midnight, the Eiffel Tower sparkles, and everyone stops to watch it. It's the most whimsical feeling you'll ever have. Everyone associates black with evil and impurity. But black is beautiful. Especially at midnight when hints of purple and blue reflect off of the moon and stars. Midnight is literally the ending of one thing and the beginning of another. How beautiful is that to think about? Without the black of midnight, there would not be a new day to dream about. That's powerful, right?

My alarm goes off, and Beyoncé pops on. "Check up on it" plays out as I try to rationalize the fact that I'm getting up so early to get my hair done. Even sweet, sweet black baby Jesus isn't up this early.

"Ari, get up, sweetie." I hear my mom's sweet voice, but I just can't get up.

"Ariana Rena, get your butt up now. You're not about to be late for this appointment." she yells up to me. I feel like this is becoming a morning ritual.

"I'm up! I'm up!" I say loud enough for me and my posters to hear. I sleep-walk into the shower and barely put my shower cap on even though my hair is about to be wet in 25 minutes. Still not quite awake after my steaming hot shower, I grab my "black girl magic" sweatshirt and some leggings and stomp down the stairs.

"Well, good morning, sunshine," my mom says to me. "Morning," I mumble back. "Let's move-we will pick up a bagel and chai on the way," she says as she scoots me out of the door.

We get to the salon, and of course, Miss Angelica is late. So, we eat our bagels and chat about the upcoming event. "We need to be out of the door by 6 so I can have you there by 6:30." my mom starts giving me directions.

"Mhmmm, Yup, okay." is about all she will let me get in. Finally, Miss Angelica shows up with her fresh wig and nails as long as my fingers. I don't know how she does hair with those nails, but nobody does it better than her. I sit down, and the miracle begins.

Three hours later, I hand Miss Angelica the money, say thanks, and hop in the car. Now I have to figure out how to spend the next 6 hours without moving my neck or eyebrows!

"Heyyyyyy, Diva!" my mom says as I hop in the car. I bat my eyes (ouch, that hurts—why must braids be so tight) and say, "Thank you, thank you," in my best Mariah Carey diva voice.

We stop and pick my outfit up from the cleaners and head home. Tonight is going to be a good night, I sing to myself.

*****

<u>10:00 a.m.</u>

I don't know where the theme Midnight in Paris came from, but I'm sure Ari put a lot of thought into it. For me, though, it means the loneliest hour of the night. All of those people who don't have a loved one just go home and cuddle up with their pillows and tears. Hopefully, one day, that will change for me so I don't have to be alone, and I'll feel free enough to show my love to someone without caring what the world sees.

I wake up dreading the hair appointment my mom has made. It's at some fancy salon and spa, and we are getting facials and our nails done. I would rather be sleeping, but I go along with it.

"Good morning, my beautiful sunshine." my mom greets me downstairs, all ready to go in her wine-colored cardigan, dark jeans, and brown leather moccasin loafers. She has perfected the modern mother look. I roll downstairs with a black hoodie with a crown on it, some jeans, and a pair of Jordans.

"Good morning, ma." I say as I grab a glass of O.J.

"We have a busy day today. How exciting! The first dance of the year. You are going to look great in your dress." she says.

"Mhmmm. Let's get out of here." I smile, trying to change the subject.

We hop in the car and blast a mix of 90s R&B. I love this music. We sing as loud as we can to TLC, Boyz II Men, and Jodeci. We skip R. Kelly and sing our hearts out to Mary J.

We pull up to the spa, and the woman greets us with beverages. A mimosa for mom and sparkling water with lime for me. My mom and I talk about everything under the sun (well, almost). I've avoided talking about Cai because if I talk about her, then she will definitely know, and I don't know if either of us is ready for it.

As we drive home, my mom puts her hand on my arm and softly caresses it. "You know you're my baby girl, right?" She's asks, "Yes, ma," I say, turning toward the window so she doesn't see the tears forming.

"I'll be here for you until the end of time, even past the point when my heart stops beating." she continues.

I say nothing and watch the trees and the buildings fly by as we drive home.

*****

<u>11:00 a.m.</u>

I love Ari's idea of midnight in Paris. It's romantic, and love is in the air. Paris is where you go to fall in love, right? I can't wait to dance the night away with Derrick, especially the slow songs, because I just love to be close to him.

"Good morning, Papa! Good morning, mami." I say as I float down the stairs, feeling like Princess Tiana.

"Good morning, baby." they both say as they're getting their stuff ready to leave.

"Erica. We will go make sure everything is being set up properly, and we will be back in time to take pictures of you and Derrick and Eric and his date. If you need anything, you call, and I will be right back here. Your auntie will be over here in a bit to do your hair and make-up." My mom says as she hurries out of the door.

My auntie is a professional hair stylist and make-up artist who has been known to beat faces so well that the gods even envy her. And lucky me, I don't have to wait for her chair. "Okay, mami." I say as I wave goodbye and turn on Netflix. I click on "Southside" and watch the Barack and Michelle love story unfold until my auntie arrives.

*****.

<u>12:00 p.m.</u>

Midnight in Paris. I remember when my mama took me to see the Eiffel Tower at midnight. It was the most mesmerizing thing I had ever seen. I couldn't stop staring at the tower because of its majestic beauty. It's something you fall in love with immediately, no matter how old you are. It's the center of everyone's attention, and it doesn't even try to be even in that moment where it lights up an entire city. It is still the same tower you admired the moment before.

"Bubs, come and eat breakfast." my mama calls up to me. As I walk toward the kitchen, I can smell bacon, and I see a big stack of blueberry pancakes waiting for me. Yum!

"Good morning," I say to my moms as they enjoy their morning coffee and tea while watching the news. "Morning, babe," my mom walks over, steals a kiss, and sits down a chai latte for me.

"Are you excited about tonight?" Nina asks as she flips another pancake.

"Yeah. I think tonight's going to be a big night." I reply.

"Well, after I'm done with this last pancake, I'm going to go get the Caddy shined up so you can arrive in style." she says as she winks at me. I laugh and stuff pancakes in my mouth and think to myself, God, please let this night turn out the way I've imagined.

*****

<u>6:00 p.m.</u>

"Ari, are you ready? We have to pick up Lia." my mom yells up the stairs.

"Yes. Coming now!" I yell back. I already know my dad is at the bottom of the stairs with his camera phone ready to roll.

I check myself out one more time in the mirror, throw up my Wakanda Forever sign, and walk to the top of the stairs.

A crisp white, fitted pants jumpsuit with a Vibranium purple lined cape jacket that only Ciara and I can pull off. The Neckline in the jumpsuit is cut just right—in style but still modest because I have no time for people to be trying to cop a peek at my goodies. And to top it off, purple strapping heels to match. My hair looks fabulous in a high ponytail braid (I still can't move my eyebrows). As I start to descend down the stairs, my dad starts to sing, "She's your queen to be...." from Coming to America, and me and my mom crack up. I hold my arms out like the future queen-to-be and let him video the entire thing, solo and all. I get to the bottom, and dad stops the video and says, "Damn, Gina." Mom hits him on the arm and says, "You are killing it, boo. My little Wakandan princess." she says as she takes my hand and twirls me.

around. "Thank ya, thank ya." I say with a Kool-Aid smile on my face.

"Okay, we have to get Lia." my mom says as she checks her watch. We both kiss my dad and say goodbye. I can already see the game starting and his snacks on the table. "Have a good time; we will see you after the dance," he says as he plops on the couch.

*****

<u>6:01 p.m.</u>

"Hey Lia. Hurry down, they will be here any minute."

"Okay. One sec." I say. I look in the mirror and say a little prayer to all my ancestors, Black and Asian. Shoot anyone at this point because I need all the good vibes I can get tonight.

I look down the stairs, and I can see my dad and mom at the bottom chatting. I start walking down, and they look up. My dad has the biggest smile, and my mom looks confused. Well, at least she's not sending me back upstairs to change.

Ari helped me pick out exactly what I wanted. A black, tailored suit, with a silk pink button-down blouse that's tailored just perfectly. We also found the perfect pair of patent leather loafers (not red bottom—a girl can still dream). My mom had the hair stylist give me a blowout that is so silky and long (and all mine) that it has.

the Real Housewives of Atlanta jealous. I'm feeling like myself again.

"You look gorgeous, sweetie." my dad says, looking at me with those kind eyes. My mom is still speechless, but when she finally comes to, she says, "That's not the dress we picked," still looking confused.

Now my dad looks confused and says, "What dress?". Now or never, Lia.

"Ma, I know you really wanted me in a dress, but honestly, I'm not really feeling dresses right now." I say.

"Oooookay, but why didn't you say something when we were shopping?" She says, frustrated.

"I didn't want to ruin your moment to see your little girl pick out a dress," I say, trying not to ruin my make- up.

"Honey, we just want you to be happy and comfortable in your own skin." my dad says.

DING DING DING!

"Mom, dad, I'm gay." I say. I don't know if I should cry or I should run. But I don't do either.

"We know, baby girl." my mom says as she walks up and engulfs me in a hug.

"And we love you more than anything in this world, no matter what," my dad adds as he joins the hug, which has now turned into a cry fest. "Thank you, Lena, thank.

you, Janelle, thank you, Rustina, thank you, thank you, B.G., and thank you, God!" I think to myself as the doorbell rings.

*****

<u>6:03 p.m.</u>

I hear the doorbell ring. "Hey, D-Money," my dad greets Derrick with this weird new nickname he's given him.

"Hi, Mr. Channing." he says, shaking my dad's hand. "Hey, D." Eric says and daps him and offers him a seat.

"The girls are still upstairs. Can I get you something to drink?" my mom offers as she comes downstairs.

"No, thank you, ma'am." Derrick answers.

"You are just so polite, Derrick. I wish Eric would learn a thing or two from you." My mom says as she pops Eric on his shoulder.

"Erica, hurry, the limo will be here any minute." she yells.

"Okay. Just getting my shoes on!" I yell down.

I tell Eric's date to go before me so they can take their pics. She walks down the stairs, and everyone oooohs and awwws at her. "Ugh," I say to myself. I look into the mirror. "Embrace what your ancestors gave you,".

I say to myself as I run my hands over my curves and start walking down the stairs.

The first person I see is Derrick, and he's smiling like he won the lottery and the pick 3. Then I spot my dad, his eyes wide, and wait, hold up...are those tears forming? As quickly as I notice them, they're gone.

"Look at my baby, looking like the Queen of the Caribbean." my mom says with a huge smile.

"Come on down here, Easy-E." my dad says with a huge smile on his face. He whispers in my ear in Spanish and hugs me, and I smile like I'm 3 years old again.

"Wow!" Derricks says as he takes my hand. "Just wow." he repeats.

"Okay, guys, let's take pictures before you're late.

*****

<u>6:15 p.m.</u>

"Russell Lee! Get down here before your Nina leaves you." My mom, Sara, yells up to me. Now, how does that even make sense? It's not like she has plans tonight, and she's not going to the dance, that's for sure.

"Okay. Just looking for something." I yell back. I can't find my bow tie. Never mind, the outfit works without it anyway.

I come hustling down the stairs, and my mama, Audra, is standing there with her phone.

"Slow down. I'm trying to get a video." She yells.

"Never mind, just go back up the stairs and come down again." she says.

"Seriously, mama!" I say, throwing my hands up.

"Yes, boy! Do what I tell you!" She says as she gives me "the look."

"Ughhh," I mumble to myself and walk back up the stairs.

"Okay. Now come," she says like she's directing a reality TV show. I walk to the top of the stairs, swing my jacket back, and put my hands in my pocket. You know, like M.J. does in Smooth Criminal (still my all-time favorite). I stand there for a second and then walk down the stairs.

"Look at my baby." Nina says from behind.

"You look good, buddy." my mom says.

"Looking for this?" my mama holds up my bow tie and smiles.

I grab it and kiss them all. My night just might go as planned.

*****

<u>6:30 p.m.</u>

Mom drops Malia and me off at the auditorium and tells us not to let the boys "get fresh" with us. What does.

173

that even mean? We just yes-ma'am her and hop out of the car.

As we walk into the auditorium, we can smell the goodness of Caribbean Paradise. We say hello to all the teachers who are volunteering and spot Miss Culver across the room. We walk over to her. "Okayyyyy, Miss Culver, you ate that!" I say. She is giving that little black dress life.

"Thank you, Ariana." she responds. "You ladies look fierce." she says with a big approving smile.

"Oh, this old thing." I say, and Malia rolls her eyes.

"Thanks, Miss C." she says.

"You look happy tonight, Malia," Miss Culver says, patting her arm.

"Yeah, my parents and I had a coming-to-Jesus moment that actually went really well." she smiles.

"That's great." Miss Culver replies, squeezing her hand, "That's really great."

"Wait, you told them?" I ask with pure excitement. "Yeah, girl. I was going to tell you before everybody got here." she says, trying to quiet me down.

"We'll see you later, Miss C." we say as we walk away.

"OMG Lia! How awesome! Tell me everything." I demand. So, we go sit in a corner, and she tells me how everything went down.

*****

<u>7:00 p.m.</u>

Everyone starts arriving and writing their request down at the DJ Booth. I decide that it will mainly be Beyoncé, but I'll let the others have a choice or two.

I see Erica and Derrick walk in, holding hands, and wave them over.

"Heyyyyyy, y'all!" I say. Erica looks like a goddess in her teal dress, and her auntie hooked up her hair and make-up. Derrick is dressed in this sleek gray suit with a teal bow tie to match his girl.

"Gon' head and do your thing, Derrick." I say to him as he walks over and shows off his outfit.

"Erica, you look AH-MAZ-ING." I say as I hug her. She grabs my hands, looks me up and down, and says, "Lupita on the Cover of Vogue ain't got nothin' on you." I smile big.

"And look at you, Lia. You look like a boss in that suit, and those shoes are everything." Erica says, grabbing Malia and hugging her.

"Thanks, gurl; you know I do what I can do every so often." Malia says with a sly smile.

The music is going on, and everyone is dancing. I see Tyler walk in with some of his Bros, and he's looking extra fine with his pink bow tie. He slides over to me, trying to look cool while he dances, and I laugh.

"Hey, Ari." he says as we dance, facing each other.

"Hey, Tyler." I smile. He leans in a bit closer and whispers, "You look beautiful." and I blush so hard that I know everyone can see it on my face.

"Thanks. You don't look too bad yourself." I say as I grab his bow tie, "You know pink is my favorite color." He gives me a mischievous smile and says, "Nope. Sure didn't."

As we dance and laugh in a circle, the music slows down to Beyoncé's X.O., and I see Malia spot Cai, who looks fabulous. The dress she is rocking just so happens to match Malia's top. By the way, neither of them knew I was scheming. I look over at Malia, who looks over at me and says something I can't quite make out, but I'm sure it started with the letter "B." I laugh, stick my tongue out, and move to the side. I see Cai walk toward Malia, grab her hand, and lead her to the dance floor. At first, there are a few looks, but after the initial surprise, everyone just goes back to dancing with their partner.

I spy Russell across the way talking to some of his friends, so I walk over to him and say, "Oh, so you can't say hey." and push his shoulder. Damn, he's getting muscles, too.

He laughs and says, "I was just watching you and your boy Tyler dance." with a smirk.

"Uh, he's not "my boy." You know a president has to mingle with the people," I say, laughing, and then I spot the bow tie. It's the color of Vibranium. My heart stops for a second, and I look up at him.

"Why are you matching me?" I say as I twirl so he can see the lining of my cape.

He shrugs and says, "Now, how was I supposed to know you would be copying me? A Diva never reveals her wardrobe, right?" He says with a smile. I look at him and say, "Mhmmmm, well, when you're ready to get your non-dancing butt on the dance floor, come and find me." I flip him the deuce sign and walk away laughing. Ooowee, he smelled good.

The night goes on, and we all dance, and we are having the best time! I'm going to have to give myself a pat on the back after the dance is over, and I can feel my feet again.

*****

<u>9:55 p.m.</u>

I hear my jam start, "Bring the beat in..." and I start dancing. Love on top is my ringtone. All of a sudden, the floor parts, "Baby, it's you," and Russell comes dancing toward me. OMG, is this really happening? Russell does the entire dance for me. It looks like he's been watching.

the video for weeks. As he gets closer, he pulls me to him and whispers in my ear, singing the song "You're the one I love..." I push him back and look at him. "You are so crazy, boy!" I smile from ear to ear. "Well, I had to get your attention somehow. No better way than with Queen Bey."

As the song ends at 10 p.m. on the dot, all the lights dim, and the Eiffel Tower lights up the entire auditorium, and he gives me the gentlest kiss on the lips.

Midnight in Paris has an entirely different meaning now.

P.S. I wonder if this is how Michelle felt when Barack kissed her after their ice cream date.

Chapter 49

Lizzo

"And the award goes to the queen of fashion, Ariana Whitaker B..."

"Ari, wake up!" Malia says as she almost pushes me off the bed and interrupts my dream.

"Whyyyyy?" I cry out like a 6-year-old who's just had her favorite stuffie ripped out of her arms.

"Listen, Diva, if Nala hadn't been between us, you would have been cuddled up on me, and you know I need my space when I sleep," Malia says as she sits up and throws off her head scarf. "Why do we have to wear these damn things?" she mutters.

"Edges, my friend," I say as I roll over with a big smile on my face.

"Ugh, am I going to have to deal with this forever?" Malia grunts as she checks her text messages.

"Whatchu talkin' bout Willis." I say as I bury my face into my pillow.

Was last night a dream? Did I actually pull off the most epic winter social ever, and did Russell seriously kiss me?

At that very moment, my phone buzzes with a text from Russell, "Good morning..."

"Good morning." I responded back and hugged my phone.

"Lawd Jesus, be a fence," Malia yells as she jumps over me to get out of bed.

"Listen, tell our friend Russell to meet us at the diner in an hour." she says as she gets her shoes on and walks out.

"I can't be ready in an hour! You know that, Lia!" I yell at her as she walks out of the door.

I flip my covers off and go into full panic mode. What do you wear after your first kiss with your best friend? What do we call each other now?

"Alexa, play Lizzo." I say as I walk to my closet; on the way, I do my hair flip and check my nails...yes, I'm feeling "good as hell." But I still have no clue what I'm going to wear. Ugh.

Chapter 50

Olivia Pope

"I'm not choosing Jake, I'm not choosing Fitz, I'm choosing Olivia."

- Olivia Pope, Scandal.

"Hey… Everybody…" I say as I walk into the diner and spot Malia, Cai, Derrick, Erica, Eric, Russell, and… Tyler. This is awkward as I look back and forth between Russell and Tyler, who are both just staring at me.

"Hey, girl. Come join us, finally." Erica says as she points at the seat between Russell and Tyler.

As I take my seat, I'm reminded of Olivia Pope. She is a fixer, and she takes no prisoners. But she has obstacles—boys—smart, good-looking boys. Do I want obstacles?

"Hey." I say to Russell as I blush.

"Hey." he says back, blushing just as much as I am.

"Sooooo anyway. Who's starving? I know I am," Malia says and interrupts the moment.

"I'm definitely hungry." Tyler chimes in as he watches Russell and me and shakes his head in disappointment.

Why do I feel bad that Tyler looks like a lost puppy?

As we wait for our food, we chat about how amazing the Winter Social was and how no sophomore class will ever be able to top it.

"So, can we talk?" Russell leans over and whispers in my ear.

All of my insides jump. "Um, sure. Whenever is cool," I say, trying to sound nonchalant, but it doesn't work.

"Cool. I'll text you later." he says as he squeezes my arm.

At that very moment, I feel a buzz in my back pocket. I grab my phone and open up a text from Tyler, who is sitting right next to me.

"So, are you and Russ a thing now????" it says.

I look straight ahead, trying to figure out what to text back. I mean, are we "a thing"? Was that just a fleeting moment in my teenage journey?" Wait...why does Tyler care?

"Noneya." I text back. I know, very mature, but that's all I could come up with.

"Oh, my bad." He replies back and shoves his phone in his back pocket, a little too aggressively for my taste.

"Alrighty, guys. I'm exhausted, and I have homework to do," I say as I scoot back from the table.

"You look way too cute to be going home and doing homework." Malia says as her eyebrows raise.

Listen. I didn't know what to wear. Maybe the black crop top with a great picture of Janet Jackson from her Rhythm Nation tour, with my leather jacket paired with a long purple African print skirt, and a pair of ankle-high leather boots with kitten heels was a bit much. But what if my second kiss was coming? I didn't want to look like I just rolled out of bed. I'm a teenager. I have teenage thoughts and teenage insecurities. Ugh! "Your girl is always cute." I say as I push in my chair and throw up the deuces.

I step out into the fresh air and take a deep breath. I'm trying not to walk back in and call Lia out on her comment.

"Hey. You ok?" I hear Russell say as he walks up behind me.

"Yeah. I'm good." I say as I pretend like I'm reading a text.

"Don't let Lia get under your skin." he says as he puts his hand on my shoulder.

"Child boo. I'm not worried about her." I say, waving the idea off even though it's not going away.

"Hey. You wanna go see a movie next weekend?" He asks.

"Yeah, that sounds like fun." I reply as I look up into his big brown eyes and lean toward him.

"Hey! I thought you were going home to do homework." Tyler says as he walks toward us.

"I am, dad!" I say, feeling extra annoyed. "I'm just waiting on my mom."

"Mhmmm," he says as he walks toward the mall. "Have fun doing homework." he gestures as he walks away.

"Ok. So, I'll text you later then." Russell says as he follows Tyler.

"Yeah. Ok. Sounds good. Have fun." I say, feeling a little deflated.

"Ari, will your mom drop me off at the gym on our way home?" Malia says before she hugs and kisses Cai on the cheek.

"Sure..." I say, feeling jealous.

"See ya!" Derrick, Eric, and Erica say as they walk toward the mall to hang out with Tyler and Russell.

"Go ahead without me, you two." Erica says as she walks toward me.

"Hey, are you alright?" She asks.

"Yeah. I'm Gucci girl." I say with a fake smile.

"Listen, chica. You are not about to lie to me." She says with a hint of that accent.

"Ok. Ok. Ugh. So, you already know what happened at the dance last night, and I'm just dying to get my head straight, and then I have Tyler texting me and looking all lost puppy." I blabber.

"Hold up. Hold up, hold up... Mr. Teen magazine, Tyler Manning, is also crushing on you. Well damn, all that Olivia Pope power is causing you some issues, huh." she says, amused. "Well, who's it going to be, Fitz or Jake?"

"Uhhhhhh...I like Russell. I think. But Tyler is cool. But I... Ugh...I don't do obstacles." I say as my mom pull up.

"Obstacles, huh? Well, I guess you better be a fixer then." she says as she hugs me.

"Let's go, Lia." I say as I hop in the car.

Yeah, how am I going to fix this? "I'm looking way too cute to be going home to do homework." I think to myself as my mom pulls away from the diner.

Chapter 51

Brandy

*"It may not be the best in someone else's eyes,
but it's the best I can do."*

- Brandy Norwood.

I love to go through my mom's music playlists because she has everything so perfectly organized. I click shuffle on her playlist entitled High School Sweetheart and lay back on my bed because homework is just not getting done at the moment.

First up: Brandy, sitting up in my room… OK, I'll give it a try. I like Brandy. I start bobbing my head, wishing this 90s music would come back... "OH MY GOD. Is this song real? Is Alexa spying on me?" I think to myself while looking around my room.

"Brandy is literally singing about my life right now..." Sitting up in my room, back here thinking about you, I must confess I'm a mess for you..."

"Every time you smile, I get tremors in my heart." Ugh.

I just can't deal with this right now. I am president of the 10th grade class of Ruth Bader Ginsberg. I have a

4.25 GPA; I am in the Math club, French club, Black Lives.

Matter club, Kids Against Guns, Future Leaders of America, and the Girl Scouts. Yes, I'm still a Girl Scout. Do not judge!

I have no time for obstacles. I have no more room on my plate. I was fine judging; I mean advising everyone else's relationships. I'm a fixer...I'm not a teenage girl who's getting tremors over some kid's smile. But it is a nice smile, a very cute smile that lights up the room whenever he's around.

Snap out of it, Ari! Where is my Whitney Houston fairy godmother, who can give me quirky advice and bippity-boppity-boos me out of this with her amazing and soulful vocals?

My thoughts are interrupted when I get a text from Russell, "Hey, can you talk now?"

"Yeah. Call me in 10. I need to find a new playlist," I responded.

"Uhhh, OK..." he responds back.

Brandy was lucky she had Whitney as her godmother.

Chapter 52

Barack Obama

Well, Ari is acting weird. I need to get my words together, or she's going to shoo me off like Michele did to Barack when he first came around.

I mean, I'm a good guy, right? I'm smart and confident; I have pretty good skin thanks to my genes; I have a 4.15 GPA, and I'm cultured. I like Biggie Smalls and Garth Brooks. I play sports, and I'm a self-proclaimed feminist, aka I shut up when Ari, Erica, or Malia speaks.

Has it been 10 minutes yet? Did she mean like 10 minutes on the dot or about 10 minutes? OK, it's been 8 minutes; I call now… "Hello," Ariana says.

Goodness: I love her voice. I get tremors in my chest.

"Hey. What are you doing?" I say, smiling way too big.

"Nothin. Just sitting in my room." she says hesitantly.

I hope she's been thinking about me because I've certainly been thinking about her non-stop since we kissed.

"Oh, cool. Me too..." I say.

"So..." we both say at the same time and laugh nervously.

"OK. So, I wanted to make sure you were OK with me kissing you last night," I blurt out.

Silence. Oh, no silence.

"Yeah..." she says, sounding unsure.

"Um, OK...I mean, I didn't ask you, and I don't want you to feel like I was..."

"Russell, stop! This isn't a me-too moment. I did not mind you kissing me. It was nice," she says, sounding much more confident in her answer.

"OK, OK, cool." I say, feeling much more confident in my decision to kiss her.

"So, what do we do now?" I ask.

"Boy! I don't know! You kissed me," she responds exasperated.

"Oh, yeah, OK...well, why don't we take it slow, no labels, and just see what happens?" I say, feeling a little deflated because I want to ask her to be my girlfriend, but I haven't had a "real" girlfriend before. Making out with Katherine McCarty in 8th grade in the movies and holding hands in the hallways for 3 weeks doesn't count.

"Yeah, we can do that. You know I just have a lot of stuff on my plate and... yeah, that sounds good, slow sounds good," I say, hoping he will want to kiss me again.

"OK, cool. Slow. Can I kiss you again?" I ask.

"Yes..." I answered, laughing at him. He's cute but still such a dork. But at least I know my best friend is a gentleman.

"OK. Well, I better go. I actually have homework, and I'm not looking too cute to do it," I say, attempting to flirt and let her know she did look really cute at brunch.

"Oh, OK, you got jokes." I say, "Talk at ya later, bubs."

"OK, Ri-Ri, see you tomorrow before school." I say and hang up.

Even my man Barack Obama had to put in the work to get Michele.

Chapter 53

Boyz II Men

"Tyler!" My mom says as she knocks on the door.

"Ma'am." I respond as I'm trying to do my homework, but it's not working.

"Hey...din...oh, I love that song." my mom says as she starts singing. "I'm down on bended knee."

"Uh, ok mom. Don't you have some Mozart or Carole King to listen to?" I say jokingly.

"Whatever, kid. Your mother knows a lot more about music than you think." She says, looking nostalgic.

"Anyway. I came to tell you dinner is ready and wanted to know why you're walking around all gloomy today and why you aren't listening to your usual rap music," she says with a knowing look.

"What are you talking about? I'm good, mom. And I listen to more than just rap. Boyz II Men is one of my favorites when I just want to chill. Anyway, I'm Just ready for lacrosse season to get here," I lie, knowing that I'm thinking about that kiss between Russell and Ari and wishing it would have been me.

"Mhmmmm. Well, I'm here if you want to talk." she says as she walks out of the room.

"Oh, by the way, Ariana's dad has an exhibit opening next week. Would you like to go with me?" She says with a smile.

"Um, sure. I'll think about it." I say, trying to play off my excitement to spend some time with Ari.

"Okey, dokey, Sweetie. Hurry down because your father has a flight after dinner." She says as she closes my door.

Of course, he has a flight. When doesn't he have a flight somewhere? Do I even have a dad? Does he even know I was MVP this year?

"Hey. What are you up to?" I text Ari because she's probably the only one who can understand.

Chapter 54

All Lives Matter

Now, let me tell you that I am the president of BLM in my school, and my membership is growing every day. I have two dozen black kids, Hispanic kids, and, of course, white kids who like to hop on the bandwagon for social issues.

Today, I'll be bringing up the issue of LGBTQIA+ rights being stripped left and right. An injustice to one is an injustice to all, and I'm not about to sit around and not do anything.

"Hey, Mrs. Culver." I say as I walk into history.

"Hello, Miss Whitaker." she responds.

"So, we have a BLM meeting today after school, and I was wondering what we could do to help bring attention to LGBTQIA families that are being attacked every day?" I say as I sit down in the empty classroom.

"Hmmmm...that's a very heavy thing to take on, but I think I have some ideas." she responds.

"As a matter of fact, our lesson on the Holocaust is going to start today, so I recommend you pay close attention. Because maybe you'll come up with some ideas on your own.".

"Bet." I respond, thinking this is actually one topic I won't know more about than Mrs. Culver.

As everyone walks into the room, I'm trying to pretend that I'm not looking for.

"Hey, Ari." I hear, walking up from behind me.

"Hey, Tyler. What's good?"

"I just wanted to say thanks for chatting with me last night." he says as he sits to my left.

Why is Tyler sitting next to me?

"Uh yeah, no biggie! I totally get what you're going through. I'm happy that my dad is actually going to be local for the next few months, so I can see him," I say as I see Russell walk in.

"Yeah, my mom told me about that." he responds.

"Hey. Madam President." Russell says as he sits to my right and gives me that Bronny Jr. smile.

"Hey, hey." I say, trying not to show that I'm blushing.

"What's good, everybody?" Malia says as she swaggers into class with Cai.

"Hey." I say immediately, saving myself from the awkward moment I'm sitting in between.

"Hey, y'all." Derrick says as he fake pulls out the chairs for Erica. "My beautiful queen." he says as he makes a gesture toward her seat.

My god, ya are so corny.

"Ok, well, I'll talk to you later." Tyler says as he gets up and makes his way back to his seat.

"Cool. I'll see you at the BLM meeting." I say, knowing there is a 50/50 chance he's going to be there.

"Yeah, I'll be there for sure." he says and winks. My tummy gets butterflies.

"So, what's the plan for the meeting?" Russell interrupts the flurry but starts another one as he puts on his glasses for class.

My goodness, he is fine.

"I'll tell you at lunch." I say as Mrs. Culver starts class.

"Good morning, ladies and gentlemen. Today, we will begin to learn about the Holocaust and World War II."

This is going to be hard to get through, but I promised I would focus because I have other lives to worry about at the moment.

Chapter 55

Jahana Hayes

"Your journey is not determined by where you begin."

- Congresswoman Jahana Hayes.

Going through my Twitter feed, I fall upon Congresswoman Jahana Hayes' page, and I decide to scroll through when I see her tweet about Transgender kids being attacked. She is so awe-inspiring and brilliant; she always looks fierce, and when she speaks, you listen. She's definitely Black Girl Magic!

I start writing out notes for the meeting and how I think we should make mass calls to our legislators or start a mass letter-writing campaign. Also, make sure we educate our peers and hand out flyers about the legislation being proposed all over the country. Listening to Mrs. Culver today got me really fired up, and it's also helping me keep my mind off of my 2 obstacles.

"Hey, girl," Malia says as she sits down at the lunch table.

"Hey!" I say with a smile, still feeling some type of way about her calling me out.

"Do you want to go see a movie this weekend? Cai has an indoor track meet, so I'm free." She says as she dips her french fries in ranch.

"Oh. Um. Russell asked me to the movie this weekend?" I say, feeling butterflies and bad for not telling her earlier.

"Oh. Ok. No big deal." she says, sounding disappointed.

"Well, I'm sure he won't mind you coming. Hello, we are all friends, and I'm sure he probably invited someone else." I say, trying to cheer her up.

"Hey, ladies." Russell says as he joins us. "Hey." I say, scooting a little closer to him. He notices and does the same.

"Oh hey! Malia was going to hit up the movies this weekend, too. I told her she could just go with us," I say, smiling way too big because I feel guilty for some reason.

"Oh. Yeah. That's cool." he says, trying to play off his disappointment.

"What's this I hear about the movies?" Erica says as she walks up with Derrick, who is carrying both of their trays. Boy, does she have him whipped.

"Yeah. We are going to hit the movies this weekend if you guys want to go." Russell says, trying to sound excited about the group outing.

"Hey, count me in." I hear Tyler say as he walks up to the table. At the same time, I feel Russell slide a little closer to me.

"Uh, ok. So, we can all meet around 6." I say, trying to figure out why I just let my potential date turn into a group function.

"Hey, Ari. What time is the meeting today?" Tyler asks.

"4 p.m. in Mrs. Culver's room." I say with a smile.

"Cool. I'll see you guys there," he says as he walks back to his side of the cafeteria.

"Oh, so now Tyler is coming to BLM meetings," Malia says, giving me the side-eye.

"I guess." I say, shrugging my shoulders.

"Ok. I'll see you after school." Russell says, giving me a weird look.

"Yeah. See you after school." I responded.

Chapter 56

Dorothy Pittman Hughes

Did I ever mention that besides all of my Beyoncé posters, I have a huge poster of Dorothy Pitman Hughes and Gloria Steinem hanging on my wall? You ask, who is Dorothy Pitman-Hughes? Well, she is one of the aunties of the Black Feminist movement. Most people talk about Angela Davis, another Badass Diva, but most don't know anything about Dorothy. Hughes sought to make the lives of ordinary women better by working to empower communities to meet their needs—whether that was childcare, recognition of Black women's inherent beauty, access to economic resources, or local healthy food.

I believe in God, but let me tell you, those two women are my Goddesses on Earth. They are the mothers of feminism and intersectionality. I know that because my mom has been telling me since I could walk.

"Hi, everyone! Please come in and sit." I say as people walk in, chatting about their day.

"Hey Ari, can you come here real quick?" Russell says as he gestures to me toward the door.

"Um…" I say as I walk behind him out of the door.

Then boom...just like that, he takes my hand and swoops in and kisses me. This time, he is more anxious.

but still super soft. Who knew those plump lips would pay off for Russell?

I smile as soon as his lips touch mine and let him hold there for a second before I push away.

"Russell Lee. What the what!?!" I say faking offense.

"I've been waiting all day to do that." he says, giving me his sly side smile.

I laugh. "Oh yeah. You couldn't have done it yesterday when I was looking extra cute instead of me in leggings and a sweatshirt that says, 'Sorry I'm late. I didn't want to be here'?"

"Ha. The great man, Aubrey, says he prefers his women in sweats with no make-up on." he says, trying to be slick.

"Whatever, boy!" I say and blush. "I have an important meeting to conduct, and you're making me late."

"Oh well, I was just taking the cue from your sweatshirt." He smiles as he walks back into the meeting.

"Whatevs." I say and push him to the side.

"Hey, y'all. Let's get this meeting started." I say as I try to wipe the smile off my face.

Chapter 57

Black Lives Matter

- Marian Anderson, American Opera Singer.

When I first saw #BLACKLIVESMATTER pop-up on my Twitter feed, I was instantly in. Today's youth sits in front of some type of screen, whether on our phones, the iPad at our desk, or at home watching the news; we are constantly bombarded with Breaking News. So, I've witnessed a multitude of murders of black men, women, and children. And to top it all off, no one wants to talk to us about it. Adults think if they just push it to the side, we will, too.

Well, luckily for me, my parents, being historians in their own right, don't push these things to the side. We talk about all of it. Though I'm afforded many privileges, I am not afforded white privilege, no matter how famous my dad is or how many accolades my mom has hanging on the wall, and no matter how well I do in school... I'm just a black girl in a white world.

I understand it as much as I don't want to understand it, as much as I want to push it to the side. It's.

just the reality of my life. But by no means does that mean I'm going to sit around wallowing. Sh*t, I'm 15 and have an entire lifetime to live and have the brains and braun to change the world, piece by piece.

"Mrs. Culver, did you get a chance to look over the flyers?" I ask, not paying attention to the fact that a tall, dark-skinned man with the smile and body of Omari Hardwick is in the room.

"Well, good morning, Miss Whitaker." she says with a smile on her face. Not her typical smile either. I recognize that smile. That is just eww.

"Ariana." she says.

"Oh yeah." I say, trying to bring myself out of my dream-like state.

"Hi. Ariana, right? I'm Dante Culver." he says, smiling.

"Um. Yes. Ariana. Ariana Whitaker." I stutter out.

"Ok. Mrs. Culver. I will pick you up after school." he says as he kisses Mrs. Culver on the cheek.

"Yes. I'll see you then." she says as she walks him to the door.

"I see you, Mrs. Culver." I say as I sit down and admire Mr. Culver's shadow.

"Girl, bye." She laughs, coming out of character for a split second.

"Now, what can I help you with?" she asks as she transitions back into teacher mode.

"Oh yeah. So, what did you think about the flyers? And can we use your classroom to have students drop off their letters? I ask about going back into BLM President mode.

"The flyers are great, and of course, I will set up a box for the letters and will even volunteer to mail them at the end of next week." she says.

"Nice job, Miss Whitaker," she says with a proud smile.

Changing the world takes more than social media rants. It takes action and people coming together to serve a common purpose.

Chapter 58

Ari and Malia,
aka Oprah and Gail

*"[I] know at all times I have somebody
that I can count on always."*

- Gayle King.

Ugh. I saw Russell and Ari hiding out kissing in the hallway before the BLM meeting. I'm just not sure how I feel about this. I mean, we have been "The Crew" since we were kids with no teeth, running around at play dates and birthday parties, playing co-ed soccer together; our families have even vacationed together for years. I just feel like it's messing up the vibe.

I mean, I know Erica has Derrick, and I have Cai, but still, they aren't the Crew. And now Russell and Ari are trying to plan movie dates alone. Since when do we go to the movies without each other?"

Ari is Oprah. She leads the group, and we follow, and that's how it's always been. I think it's because she is the shortest, so she has a bit of a complex. But still, it works for all of us.

I'm here, Gayle. I make sure I'm by her side. Yeah, I'm allowed to do my own thing, but I'm always by her side. But if Russell is playing Stedman, where do I fit?

"Hey Lia!" Cai says as she grabs my hand after school.

"Hey," I say.

"Well, damn girl! Happy to see you, too." she says sarcastically.

"My bad. I was just thinking..." I say, kissing her on her cheek as we walk into the gym.

"What's up?" She asks as she leads me over to the bleachers.

"Nothing. I mean, nah, nothing," I say, turning to her and smiling. "How was your day? You excited about your meet this weekend?" I ask.

"Omg, I'm so nervous. You know how many colleges will be there, ugh." she says, throwing her leg over mine and sitting back.

"You'll be great," I say, sitting back with her. "You're one of the best in the state. You got this." I grab her hand and squeeze it.

"Thanks, bae," she says. "Hey, you want me to rebound for you?" She asks, jumping up and passing me the ball.

"Yeah. Thanks," I say.

She always knows how to make me feel better. I bet Gayle probably has a side boo when O isn't around.

Chapter 59

Tyler Perry

*"Don't wait for someone to green light your project;
build your own intersection."*

- Tyler Perry.

"Ari! Russell's here." My mom yells from downstairs.

"Okay," I yell as I'm putting on my lip gloss.

I love Tyler Perry movies, not for the cinematic brilliance but rather because they feel like home. When we go down to Atlanta and visit family, I fall right into a Tyler Perry movie. They think we are the bougie part of the family, and my mom hates that stereotype, but my cousins and I have the best time running around. I'll obviously apply to Spelman, even though my parents think I'm definitely going to Howard.

I run down the stairs and see my mom and Russell chatting. He's wearing a black sweater that fits him just right, dark jeans, and Timberlands, and it looks like he just got a fresh cut.

"Hey there." I say, trying to sound normal because my parents don't know that we are a thing or maybe not a thing; they definitely don't know we did a thing, not that thing. Anyway, in their eyes, we are strictly platonic. And.

I'm not going to say any different until we figure out what this thing is.

"Hey," he says with that big smile. "Are you ready?

Nina is waiting."

"Yeah, just let me grab my jacket." I say. Winter came in like a hawk this year. It was still nice outside last week at the Winter Social, but all of a sudden, Mother Nature decided the sun needed to rest, and now it's brick cold.

"Have fun, you guys." my mom says. "Ari, don't forget we are decorating for Christmas tomorrow, so be back by 10."

My mom likes to decorate before Thanksgiving for some reason. It's always been our tradition to do it the Sunday before Thanksgiving. So, I just go with it.

"Okay, mom." I say as I walk out of the door.

"Hi, Nina." I say as I jump into the car.

"Hi, Ari." she replies.

"Lia should be running out any minute." I say, wondering why she didn't get her dad's punctuality.

"I think I might sneak into the movies with y'all." She says, looking in the rear-view mirror and spotting the horrified look on Russell's face.

"Seriously, Nina!" he says, not hiding his dismay.

"Well, never mind then, I guess." she says, sounding offended, but her smile is betraying her. OMG, does she know?

"What's poppin?" Malia says, interrupting my thoughts.

"Hey." we all say, as she forces me to the middle of the seat.

"I'll be back right after the movie to get y'all." she says as we pull up to the theater.

"Thanks, Nina!" We all say as we pile out of the car.

"What's good, bruh?" Tyler says as he sees Russell and does some weird handshake.

"Hey, Ari." he says and just nods his head toward me.

"Uh hey..." I say back, wondering what the weird, nonchalant nod was for.

"Hey, hey, hey!" Erica says, walking up and holding hands with Derrick.

"I'll grab the popcorn." Malia says, nudging me to walk with her.

"I'll go with her." I say and give Russell a look.

"Oh, hey, do you want..."

"No, no, we got this." Malia interrupts him and grabs my arm.

"So, how are thingsss?" Malia says teasingly.

"Things are good." I say. I'm not falling for this trap.

"So, are you and Russell a thing?" She asks.

"Girl, I don't know. We are just keeping it light and free." I responded.

"Mhmmm. Well, you know Tyler is jonesing for you, right?"

"What are you talking about? No, he is not." I say, looking over at Tyler, who's pretending like he's not looking in our direction.

"Anyway, I heard him, and Sloane might be a thing." I say, rebutting her accusation.

"Ha. Last time I checked, Sloane and I were playing for the same team, so that's not happening." she says with a smirk.

"Girl, for real? Have you ever." I start asking.

"Hell no!" she interrupts. "Only Cai."

"Oh, okay, my bad..." I say. "Well, how's that going?"

"Good. We're Gucci," she says unconvincingly. "I mean, her parents still don't know, and my parents think I just figured it out, so I can't possibly be with anyone. But other than that, it's good." she says, sounding a little confused about whether she's good or not.

"Well, that's a start. You guys will figure it out." I say, trying to reassure her.

As we sit down for the movie, I see seats open in our row. One between Tyler and Russell and one between Russell and Erica. Right as I'm about to step over Tyler to sit between Russell and Erica, Malia yells as she bumps me into the seat between Russell and Tyler, "Hey E. Thanks for saving my spot; you know I like to be right in the middle of the screen."

"Excuse you," I say as I regain my balance.

I hear a snicker and see her smile as she sits down.

As we all get settled in and the lights start to go down, I try to inch a little closer to Russell. He feels what I'm doing and inches a little closer himself. Our shoulders are touching, and I'm loving this shoulder connection.

About midway through the movie, I reach into the popcorn bucket at the exact same time as Tyler. I immediately try to pull my hand back, but he holds it there for a second. I try to act like it's not awkward, and at the same time, I feel a little tingle. I look toward him, and he has a slight smile on his face. OMG, what is going on right now? I immediately scoot closer to Russell, hoping he didn't notice popcorn-gate. He didn't, of course, because he was laughing hysterically at the movie. Phew!

The movie gets over around 8:45, and everyone wants to go grab an ice cream afterward. Malia and I decided to share a cup of cake batter with extra chocolate sauce. We've been sharing that since we discovered it at the age of 5. We all sit down and chat until Russell's grandma picks the 3 of us up. We wave goodbye, and of.

course, I'm in the middle again, which I don't mind because it's a few extra minutes getting shoulder action from Russell.

"How was the movie?" Nina asks as we drive home.

"Hilarious." Russell says as he rests his hand on my thigh.

I perk up. "Yeah, it was great." I say in a squeaky voice.

Malia looks over and sees Russell's hand on my thigh and chuckles. "Yeah, hilarious." she says as she rolls her eyes.

I'm starting to think Malia is feeling some type of way about me and Russell. But why?

As we cruise down the highway, I keep feeling my phone buzz in my back pocket, but I'm trying to ignore it. I finally reach for it and see a few texts from Tyler. I sit up and read them.

"Hey! That was fun tonight. Call me later. I have something to tell you."

"Okay." I text, trying to figure out when Tyler and I became phone buddies. Like, who likes to talk on the phone when you can just text and multi-task?

We pull up to my house, and we all jump out of the car.

"Thanks, Nina." I say and turn to Russell.

"Thanks for a fun night. I'm sorry that it turned into a group outing." I say, grabbing his hand and squeezing.

"No big deal. It turned out to be a fun night." he says. Then he whispers in my ear, "I just wish I would have kissed you."

Lawd, every hair is standing on my arm. My body feels warm, and I don't know what to do.

I look down so he doesn't see all these things happening. "Yeah, me too." I say and smile as I walk off.

What in the world is happening? What are these things happening to me? It's just a kiss; Russell is just a boy. A fine, creamy boy. But last month, he was just goofy Russell. Now, he looks completely different. I try to shake off all the feelings before I walk into the house, convinced my mom will know.

"Hey boo, thang!" I hear my dad say from his office.

"Hey, daddy!" I say as I stand in his doorway.

"Your mom is sleeping. How was the movie?" He asks as he gets up to hug and kiss me on the forehead.

"It was so funny. You know Tyler Perry is the king of black family comedy." I say.

"True. True." he says.

"Well, you look extra happy." he says. My gawd, can he tell? Does he know?

"Yeah, I am. Everything is good at school, and we are planning something big for our protest.

thing." I say, trying to think about something else besides Russell.

"Good deal, my girl! Changing the world one rock at a time," he says as we both walk to our rooms.

"Night, daddy. Love you."

"Night baby girl. Love you more.".

Chapter 60

Holiday Soul

You know when a black person knows it's okay to start putting up Christmas stuff. The moment the radio station or your parents start playing the Temptations.

In my dream, I can smell bacon, and I hear "in my mind." I immediately jump and realize it's not a dream. It's time to start decorating! It's my favorite time of the year. Thanksgiving is next week, and the next thing you know, Christmas is here.

"Good morning." I say as I come down the stairs. I can see my mom swaying back and forth as she flips pancakes. I see my dad coming up from the basement with Christmas boxes singing away.

"Good morning, Ari." my mom says when she turns around and catches me stealing bacon from the table.

"Girl, if you don't get out my bacon, I know something." she yells as she smiles and walks over and steals a piece herself.

"Hold up. How are y'all both eating the bacon and I'm doing all this hard labor?" My dad says as he grabs a piece and heads back down to get more boxes.

Mom and I laugh, knowing she always has extra bacon she hides in the microwave because she knows we love to eat it while she cooks breakfast.

"Are you ready to decorate?" My mom asks, extra excited.

"Yes, ma'am!" I say with a little shimmy.

We have the best decorations. A full village with a train, an entire gang of black Santas, a Kwanzaa set up, and lots more. Once we do the outside lights and set up the other stuff, we take a break and head to the tree farm to pick a tree. I plan to continue this tradition with my future family.

"Tell your dad to come up for breakfast, please," my mom says as she sets the pancakes and the hidden bacon on the table.

"How's your stuff coming along, daddy?" I ask as I take another piece of bacon.

"Really good. Opening night is December 28th. It will be the 20th anniversary of my first exhibit." he says, looking proud.

"Wow, that's great, and dang, you're old!" I say, teasing him.

"Oh yeah. I bet I could still catch you," he says as he gets up from the table.

"Mhmmm. In your dreams." I say as I pick up my plate and take it to the table.

"Okay, you two." mom says as she sips her coffee. "Let's get this Whitaker Decorating party started. Meet you outside in 10." she says, and she puts the dishes in the dishwasher.

As I run upstairs, I can hear my phone ringing. That reminds me I need to change my ringer to something more festive.

"What it do?" I say as I answer it before it goes to voicemail.

"Hey..." Tyler says, sounding confused.

"Oh hey…" I say. Code-switching is just natural now.

"You didn't call me last night." he says.

"Oh. Sorry. Was there something super important?" I ask.

"Oh no. Just wanted to chat with you." He says.

"Oh..." I sound completely confused.

"So, what are you up to today? Wanna..."

"We are decorating for Christmas," I say, cutting him off.

"Already?" He responds.

"Yeah, it's our family tradition." I say, feeling defensive.

"Oh, okay. That's cool. Well, I'll let you get to that then." he says.

"Tyler, is everything okay?" I ask, concerned.

"Yeah, everything is great…," he says, and I can tell he's lying.

"I'll call you later. Is that cool?" I say.

"Yeah. Cool, talk at ya later." he says and hangs up. Well, that was awkward.

"Ari, let's go! Before your dad electrocutes himself!" my mom yells up the stairs.

"Coming!" I say as I throw my hair up in a cute ponytail and put on my reindeer headband. Don't judge; my mom and dad have on his and hers Santa hats.

And once again, the temptations are playing on the outside speakers. I love our traditions.

Chapter 61

Mariah Carey

"We have to go through certain things in order to appreciate life and learn lessons."

- Mariah Carey.

Finally, my song "All I Want for Christmas" by the one and only Mariah comes on as we head to pick out the tree. This is my favorite part of the day. All the lights are up, and the blow-ups in the yard are ready to go once the sun goes down. My phone buzzes, and it's a text from Russell.

"Hey. How is decorating going?" He says.

"Good. You should come over later for hot cocoa," I respond back.

"Cool. I'll check with my moms and see if it's OK. One more month until I'll have a license. Thank God." he responds back.

"Yassss! Somebody in the crew needs one ASAP!!!!"

I say.

"See ya later, maybe xoxo," I respond.

"Xoxo." he responds back.

Well, isn't that cute? I smile and think to myself.

My phone buzzes again. I hope it's another "xo," but it's Malia. Which I'm actually happy about because she's been acting weird.

"Hey, I see y'all put up the lights, so I'm going to assume it's Christmas tree time?" she writes.

"Yes, ma'am. Are you going to come over and help decorate the tree?" I ask.

"Bet. Just text me when you get back." "OK. Talk to you in a bit." I respond.

I love it when Malia helps decorate. We have the best time, and mom lets us listen to my Christmas playlist, which is mainly Destiny's Child, and some ratchet ones I found on one of my dad's old CDs.

"This is the one." I say as I spot the perfect tree.

"Seriously, Ari?" My mom says. "That's like 10 feet tall."

"Yup. That's it!" I say with a huge smile on my face. As we load up the car, I text Malia and Russell that we are on our way back. They both text back that they will be over. I'm so excited to trim the tree with my best friends.

As I'm putting the last touches on the village, the doorbell rings. Malia is all decked out in her ugly Santa sweater and a pair of Air Force Ones to match.

"Um, isn't it a bit early for the sweater?" I say jokingly.

"Girl, bye. Not when the entire neighborhood is lit up from just your house." she says.

"True." I say, laughing.

"Russell should be here soon." I say as I walk toward the kitchen to get the homemade hot cocoa started.

"You invited Russell." she says, sounding a little disappointed.

"Yeah. I didn't think you would mind. Do you?" I ask.

"I guess not. This is just usually our thing." she says with her shoulders slumped.

"I know. But it's Russell. OUR friend Russell." I say, reminding her we both like Russell every other day.

"True, but all you guys do is flirt." she says defensively.

"Wait, what? No, we don't!" I say back defensively.

"Uh yeah, you do. And you're sneaking kisses and ish." she says.

"Lia, you cannot be serious! As much as I have had to watch you and Cai, you're upset over a week of me and Russell?" I say, heated.

"Well, Cai isn't a part of the crew," she says, almost yelling.

"So, your issue isn't because I have a boy that I like, but because it's Russell?" I say, my eyes stinging. What is.

her problem?

"Exactly! What if you guys don't work out? What happens then?" She lowers her tone and sounds sad.

"We haven't even gotten to a place to be called anything, so we will always be friends." I say, trying to sound reassuring but secretly worried about what she said. What if it doesn't work out? Malia and Russell are my best friends in the whole entire world.

"Whatever, yo!" She says as she walks back out to talk to my parents.

I sit in the kitchen feeling deflated. Why can't she just be happy for me? Why can't she hope for the best? I like Russell. He likes me. We will always be friends. Won't we?

"Ari. Russell's here!" my dad yells from the foyer. I immediately perk up when I see his smile.

"Hey." he says as he walks toward me, decked out in an Adidas sweatsuit and a hat.

"Hey." I say, wishing I could just kiss him, but I can't because my dad is literally standing right behind us.

At that very moment, I hear Mariah's voice and know it's a sign. All I want for Christmas is Russell, well, and tickets to Beyoncé and... Never mind, you get the point. Malia needs to stop worrying because it will all work itself out no matter what happens between Russell and me.

Chapter 62

Love & Basketball

"I've been in love with you since I was eleven, and it won't go away."

- Sanaa Lathan - Monica Wright

"Tyler. Are you ready?" My dad calls up to me. "The limo will be here any minute."

"Yeah. Just a second." I say as I fix my tie. I absolutely hate these events. It's all for photo ops, so my dad can be seen as the good family man. The funny thing is I have seen my dad twice this entire month, and that's when he was packing his bag to go back out on the road. My mom acts like she's not bothered by it, but I can tell it's wearing on her now. But she says we have to support each other and see the bigger picture, which means going to events where I spend most of my time with a smile plastered to my face, bored out of my mind.

"There's my boy." my dad says as I come down the stairs.

I roll my eyes and say, "You realize the Duke basketball game is on tonight, right?"

He laughs. "Don't worry. I have someone sending us updates.".

This is the dad I miss. The guy who would rush home and watch a game with me. Now, he's all business, events every week on top of all of his other Senate stuff. I miss my dad.

I'm happy I have Ari to talk to. Her dad is gone all the time, too. I wonder what she's doing now? I should text her. I hope she doesn't think it's weird that I text her. Ever since our project, I just wanted to hang out with her and get to know her better. Some days, she's all I think about. Anyway, she won't answer me about her and Russell, so I guess that means I can at least talk to her until she tells me otherwise.

Hey...maybe she will come over and watch basketball with me. Yeah, I should definitely text her.

My mom walks from behind the corner in a beautiful blue gown. "You look very beautiful, Mrs. Manning," my dad says as he kisses my mom on the cheek. I've learned you don't get to kiss girls on the lips once they have applied their lipstick. Which I think is bogus. Hello, they have an entire stick of the stuff.

"Thank you, Mr. Manning." she says.

"Tyler, you know we are missing the Duke game." she says, sounding as agitated as I feel. She's become my new basketball buddy.

"You, too, are incredulous. Have a little faith in the old man." he says as he opens the door for us.

We laugh, but all I can think about is Ari and how I wish I could chill with her and listen to her chatter away about social injustices and basketball. I love my bro, Russell, but I really like Ari, too. I don't know what to do.

"I hope this limo has a TV because tip-off is in 5 minutes." I say as I put on my coat and follow my parents to the limo.

Chapter 63

The First Amendment

"The truth is, no one of us can be free until everybody is free."
- Maya Angelou.

The First Amendment states: Congress shall make no law respecting an establishment of religion, or prohibiting the free exercise thereof, or abridging the freedom of speech, or of the press; or the right of the people peaceably to assemble, and to petition the government for a redress of grievances.

Therefore, I asked Principal Markowitz if we could hold a sit-in on the same Wednesday we are mailing in our letters to protest against the family separation. Let me tell you something about my school administration. They are full believers of our constitutional rights. Each year, we have a speaker from one of the many law schools and the Congress come in and speak to us about the Constitution and current laws and rulings. They allow us to have a dialogue and voice our opinions respectfully, of course. We don't all agree, which is fine, but none of us can say we aren't fully aware of the world around us. That's why I stan for RGB Prep and Principal Markowitz.

"Hi, Mrs. Culver." I say as I walk into her class before school.

"Good morning, Miss Whitaker." she says, looking at her computer. She looks upset, which is unlike her.

"What's the tea, Mrs. Culver." I say as I step toward her desk.

"Oh, Ariana...I just don't get our world today." she says, sounding deflated. Wow, she never calls me by my first name.

"There was another school shooting yesterday." she looks up at me with sadness in her eyes.

"Yeah. I saw." responding, feeling angry.

"When is enough enough?" she says, and she closes her laptop.

"I hear ya. When will it matter." I say. I know what our next letter-writing campaign and sit-in will be about. Not that it will change anything, but we have to voice our concerns until they do hear us.

"So, what can I do for you?" She sighs, giving me her full attention.

"I just wanted to check in on the letters and make sure we are good to go after lunch for the sit-in," I say, refocusing myself.

"Yes, ma'am. We got over 100 letters turned in, and I'm going to send them off today. We will also meet right in the common area after lunch, and Principal

Markowitz has approved 10 minutes." She answers as she prepares for her first class.

"You guys are so fortunate to have a principal who hears and sees you as young adults and future leaders. I wish I had been afforded the same space and voice during my young adult years. Never take this for granted," she says as she looks over her shoulder.

"Great. And I know. Principal Markowitz is a G, and I'll make sure these moments are worth it. You're a G, too, Mrs. Culver. Thank you for everything you do." I say as I walk out.

Chapter 64

No Justice, No Peace

"The greatness of a man is not in how much wealth he acquires, but in his integrity and his ability to affect those around him positively."

- Bob Marley.

Before lunch, I remind everyone that we are having the sit-in in the common area. Everything should be peaceful, I remind them. The senior class president, Zanai, has volunteered to oversee the moment of silence, and the teachers who are on their break have volunteered to chaperone the moment so it doesn't get out of hand.

"Hey, Ari." Tyler says as he walks up to our table at lunch.

"Hey, Tyler. Make sure you and all your bros make it after lunch." I say, smiling.

"Don't worry, Chica. We will all be there to support you. But are you giving anything away?" He asks.

As I start to curse him, he stops me. "I'm just kidding. We will be there." He says as he winks at me and walks away.

"You and Tyler have a thing." Erica says.

"Yeah." Derrick agrees.

"Um, no, we do not have a thing. He gets on my last good nerve." I say, trying to end this conversation before Russell gets back to the table.

"Don't let Russell hear you say that." Malia chimes in.

"Oh, my bad," Erica says. "What's going on with you and him anyway?" she asks.

"We are just..." I begin to say what we are when Russell walks up and interrupts.

"What's good, crew?" he says.

Everyone moves in their chair, uncomfortable.

Yeah, that's not awkward, I think to myself.

"Nada." I say, trying to act normal.

"Hey, is everyone ready for the sit-in?" I say, bringing the subject back to the topic at hand.

"Yup. Got my phone ready so we can put it on snap, Twitter, and TikTok," Malia says.

"Good deal." I say, happy to have friends that support me.

The bells ring, and we all make our way to the common area.

Tyler walks up beside me.

"Hey. How was your dad's event last night? You looked nice all GQ in your tie." I say as I try to make my way to the podium.

"Boring. Missed half of the game." he says as he continues to walk with me.

"Oh, that sucks. Duke killed them." I say as I walk up and say hello to Zanai.

"Well, maybe you can come over and watch the next one." he says as he stands there.

"Um, ok. Yeah. Maybe." I say awkwardly.

"Cool. Good luck with this thing. A lot of people seem to be showing up." he says as he walks back to his group.

Now that he mentions it, there are a lot more people than I thought would show up. And did Tyler just invite me over to his house?

"Hello Fellow Dissenters" Principal Markowitz says on the microphone, interrupting my thoughts.

"Please be seated," she continues. She lays out the ground rules of the sit-in and explains the importance of everyone's First Amendment rights to protest and not to shun or shame anyone who decided not to participate.

"Ariana Whitaker will now tell you why you are here today, and you will have 10 minutes after your moment of silence." she says as she steps away.

"Good morning," I say into the microphone, and of course, it makes that high-pitched sound.

"Today, we are here to protest…" I say and continue to give my speech, which is Michele Obama worthy for a 15-year-old.

"And as the incredible Dr. MLK, Jr. said, "No justice, no peace." As soon as I end my speech, all of a sudden, Russell raises his fist and starts chanting, "No justice. No Peace!" and the entire common area follows his lead. I can't tell you how proud I am at this moment. Especially since not one person turned it into a circus, and some of the teachers even participated in the chant.

After everyone calms down, Zanai does the moment of silence for the individual suffering from the current political circumstances we are living through daily. We all sit there as a united front of young people for the next 10 minutes.

Ten minutes may not seem like a long time, but to many, it can feel like an eternity.

Think about it… Every time a parent can't reach their child during a school shooting, it feels like an eternity. Every time a family is separated trying to flee violence at our borders, it feels like an eternity. Every time a black child leaves their home and their mother and father wait for them to return safely, it feels like an eternity. Every time an LGBTQIA kid steps out into the.

world as their authentic self, not knowing what is going to happen to them, it feels like an eternity.

Ten minutes is an eternity for many.

Not every school gets to do this, but imagine if they could. Peaceful people show their civil dissonance to the world. Letting them know we will not be silent about things that affect us, our country, and our future.

No Justice. No Peace. One Love.

Chapter 65

Soul Food

"Bless this bread, bless this meat, bless this belly 'cause I's gon' eat!"

- Reverend Williams, Soul Food.

Everyone knows that the movie Soul Food is a staple during the holiday season for black families, and this Thanksgiving is no different. As my mom, dad, and both sets of grandparents chit-chat in the kitchen area, Malia and I sit down and start watching our movies for the day. Seeing as Malia comes from the "elites," her family dinner is later, so she always spends the first half of the day with me, and she gets to satisfy her soul food cravings, i.e., baked macaroni and cheese, collard greens, ham, yam...you name it.

"Girl, yesterday was awesome." Malia says as she adjusts her pillow and puts her feet up on the couch.

"I know, right? I can't believe that many students wanted to participate. I thought maybe 75 would show. But 200...that's wild." I say, feeling super proud and reliving the moment.

"I'm really proud of my bestie." she says, bumping me with her foot.

"Thanks, bestie." I say, happy that we are past that weird conversation.

I press play on the TV, and we binge-watch holiday movies.

"Ari, Lia! Time for dinner." my mom yells from the dining room.

"Oh, I'm so ready for some real food." Malia says.

"I know you are, girl," I say, knowing that at her next dinner, they will be having crudites and butternut squash soup served with salmon roe. None of which Lia eats. She's definitely a home-cooked meal kind of girl, but when your mom owns the largest black-owned law firm in the city, and your grandparents run with the elites, then you have to suffer through stuff like this.

"I know Russell feels the same way you do. I bet Nina is throwing down before they have to go to the event tonight." I say as we walk to sit down.

"Hey, you wanna go with me? I'm sure you have something in your closet, and I'm sure you wouldn't mind seeing your boo," Malia says with a sly smile.

I eye her suspiciously. "First of all, he's not my boo, and sure I'll go so we can secretly throw shade." I say, very happy I get to see my boo.

"Mom, you and Grandma and Mama G threw down." I say as I go to steal a roll.

"Aht Aht," my grandma says. "You better bow your head for grace."

I do as I'm told, just like everyone did as they were told by Big Mama in Soul Food.

Chapter 66

Bad & Boujee

"Are you ready?" Malia asks me as she walks into my room.

"Yup. Just putting the finishing touches on." I say as I add dangly earrings my mom let me borrow. No, they're not real. Brenda doesn't play that game. But they still look good.

"Well damn, Bad & Bougee...I see you, sis." I say to Malia, who is not dressed in her typical clothes. Tonight, she is rocking a coral-colored strapless dress that hugs all her little curves and shoes that I know for sure she hates walking in.

"You know how we do. You're looking pretty B&B yourself," she says back.

"Well, thank ya." I say as I do my Kenya Moore twirl. Tonight, your girl is rocking a little black dress with one sequined sleeve (the perks of wearing the same size as your mother) and a pair of black heels that I know for sure I hate walking in.

I grab my clutch, which has nothing but Carmex and my phone in it, but it matches, and we are out the door.

As I hop in the back of the car with Malia, I notice Mrs. Pat wiping her eyes and Mr. Wu sitting there looking equally unhappy.

"Uh, hi." I say, trying to clear my throat and not sound awkward.

"Hi Ari, so happy you can join us." Mrs. Pat says.

"Did you save your uncle a plate from your house?"

Mr. Wu says, trying to ease the tension, "You know there are leftovers for days, and Mama G made a sweet potato pie just for you." I say, smiling.

"That's what I'm talking about." he smiles, but there's something sad about it as he looks away.

Malia and I chatted the entire ride about school and used codenames we made up for Cai and Russell.

Did I mention I'm surprising Russell? I figured I owed him since his little surprise at the Winter Social. Also, I want to personally thank him with a tiny little kiss for his support at the sit-in.

As we pull up to the venue at the Four Seasons, I am in awe. We do events for my dad's art, but it's not usually during the holiday season, so everything isn't all sparkly and bright.

The bellman opens the car door, and Malia and I get out first and wait for her parents. Mrs. Pat looks like something out of an Essence magazine; so regal and put together, and no tears in sight. Mr. Wu looks handsome and judgely (is that a word?). You get what I'm saying. They make a very powerful-looking couple.

We all walk in together, and I immediately spot Russell. He's all dressed up in his black suit and red tie. A few seconds later, he spots me, and I bet both our smiles blinded that room.

"Lawdddd." Malia says, laughing as we start walking over to him.

"Oh, so now you're pulling up on me at parties." he says, looking faux-shocked.

"I figured I owed you a surprise." I say, trying to be flirty, but know I'm horrible at it.

"Oh, okay," he replies.

The three of us chit-chat about all the uppity people here and school. Russell mentions Tyler's dad may make an appearance, obviously for political reasons.

"Hey, come over here. Let me show you something." Russell says as people start to make their way toward the table.

I smirk and follow him. "What do you need to show me?"

"Just come on." he says as he pulls me away toward a giant room. It's all lit up and decorated for Christmas. It looks like a winter wonderland. As I look around, trying to take it all in, he grabs my hand and pulls me closer. I try to maintain even breaths, but the anticipation kills me.

I turn toward him and reach up for his face, and just as I do, he turns to me... "Ouch," he says as I poke him in the eye.

"OMG, I'm so sorry." I say as I laugh hysterically.

"Damn, girl." he says as he starts to laugh.

"Let me do it this time." he says as he leans down toward me. This time, my hand touches his cheek instead of his eye, and we kiss. ooooo, wee, let me tell you, Russell has been practicing because this was a real kiss, like a real kiss. It was everything I had hoped for and more. Lawd, give me the strength not to kiss him all the time.

"Umhmm. I hear, and I look over and see Malia.

"Uh, can y'all stop making out and come sit down before the dude with the long nose, Hayes, tries to sit down at our table." she says as she turns with her hands on her hips.

Russell and I look at each other, giggle, and walk in behind Malia.

"Did I tell you you're rocking the B&B look tonight?" He says as we sit down.

"Thank ya, kind sir." I say, faking a hair flip.

I'm happy Malia invited me to this event. It might be uppity, and there might not be any dressing and mac-n- cheese, and I might not be able to pronounce some of the things on the menu, but I got to play dress up and get a real kiss. This is a Thanksgiving I am truly thankful for.

Chapter 67

Etta James

"When I look out at the people and they look at me and they're smiling, then I know that I'm loved. That is the time when I have no worries, no problems."

- Etta James.

I wake up to Beyoncé singing Etta James's At Last, and I immediately know today is going to be a good day. Now, there is a lot of drama around Bey singing Etta, but I'm sure Etta was flattered. Etta James, one of the greatest singers of our lifetime, dealt with racism and sexism. To be a black woman is to hold on to faith so tightly you have no other choice but to fight for the good of the world. So, needless to say, if she's going to choose someone to carry on her legacy, I'm sure she would choose someone who is involved in the new movement.

I'm feeling festive today; even though it's a Monday, I'm feeling alive. I throw on an oversized Coogi sweater that shows my shoulder, a pair of black jeans, and some UGGs.

"Morning." I say as I stroll down the stairs.

"Morning, sweet pea." my mom says as she's rushing around getting her work stuff together.

"Um, are you okay?" I ask, trying to stay out of her way.

"Yes. My assistant forgot to update my calendar. I have a big meeting I need to be at in an hour, and I'm not remotely prepared at the moment because I thought I had another 6 hours." she says. She clearly is having a case of the MONDAYs.

"Yikes. I hope you forgive Tamika. I really like her, and I'm sure it was an honest mistake." I say, trying to be positive and praying for Tamika.

"Mhmmm. She's going to get an honest cursing out when I get there." she says as she kisses me and sprints out the door.

"Stay Black or die trying." I yell behind her as I eat my avocado toast. Aye, this stuff is good, so don't judge.

"Say what, Malcolm?" I hear my dad yelling from his office as I'm walking out of the door.

"Those paintings better get here from Paris by Friday, or I'll personally make a trip, and the Parisians will have another reason to dislike loud Americans." he continues.

Again, I think to myself, this is going to be a drama and stress-free day.

"Hey, Ari." Malia says, running back to her house and putting on her jacket.

"Hey Lia." I say, waiting for her to catch up so we can walk to the bus stop together.

"I cannot wait until one of us gets a license because this bus thing is for the birds." I say.

"For real, for real." she agrees.

"Yo listen, this girl keeps hitting me up in my DMs. She goes to school at Siddy and plays on their b-ball team. She's, ya know. I told her I have a girl, but dang, sometimes it feels like I don't because Cai and I have different schedules." Malia starts to tell me this on the bus ride.

"But I told her we could hang as friends. So we are going to hang at the Holiday Classic that weekend." she continued.

"Hol' up, Hol' up. Let me get this straight. A girl who's been flirting with you, who attends our arch-rival school, wants to hang with you, and you told her you have a girl but still want to hang with her." I say, looking skeptical.

"Yeah. It would be nice to have a friend who gets me on that level. Ya know." she says.

"Oh yeah. I'm not on that level? Hmmm. Okay." I say, truly offended.

"Ari! You know what I mean." she says. "Whatever." I say and walk off the bus.

"Whatever." She says behind me.

"Hey." Russell says as he walks up.

"Hey." I say, not feeling as giddy as I was earlier. "So you wanna do something after school?" He asks "Let's play it by ear." I responded.

His shoulders immediately slump. "Okkkk... everything good with you? Where's Lia?"

"I'm not Lia's keeper!" I say a little too much edge in my voice.

"Uh, okay." he says, backing away. "I'll see you later, I guess." he says, trying to gauge if I'm going to yell at him again or act somewhat normal.

"Yeah, I guess." I say as I walk away.

Today was supposed to be a good day. I didn't want any drama. Why can't people just be normal? Why does Lia need a new version of me?

Ugh! No, we didn't need a new version of At Last. Yes, I get that the new version doesn't take away from the old version. Yes, I'm still going to be petty.

I've been Monday'd.

Chapter 68

Tina Turner

"My legacy is that I stayed on course... from the beginning to the end because I believed in something inside of me."

- Tina Turner.

This week was the longest week ever. I avoided Malia as much as I could because I was too embarrassed to let her know how hurt I was about her wanting a new friend. I already had to share her with Cai. Now, some new girl has come along, and I have to share her with her, too. Russell was super sweet, though. He made me origami flowers, and we snuck a few kisses after school, and he let me rant and rave about Malia. He's a keeper, for sure. I don't know exactly what I'm keeping him for, friend or more, but he's definitely a keeper.

I walk down stares in my sequined pink slippers and my nightshirt that says "I'm dreaming of a Black Christmas" with a Black Santa and Frosty the Snowman dappin' it up. As I get closer to the kitchen, I can hear mom blasting Tina Turner. Like I said, it's been a rough week for the Whitaker household, so who else would you blast at unhealthy levels on a Saturday morning but the rising Phoenix of rock and soul? If you don't know about

Anna Mae, aka Tina Turner, then are you even Black? Shoot, are you even from the planet Earth? Even Aliens.

know who Tina is. The trials and tribulations Tina went through to come out on top like she did. She deserves nothing but respect and gratitude, and Angela Bassett gracing us with her presence and bringing it all to life, making Black cinematic history. Tina and Angela deserve all the flowers.

"Good morning." my mom says as she taps her toes and snaps her fingers to the beat while making pancakes.

"It is definitely Mornin'." I sigh, trying to find the motivation to get over the week.

"Wanna talk about it?" She asks as she sets a big stack of pancakes with strawberries and whipped cream in front of me. She always knows what I need.

"It's not that deep." I say as I cut into the fluffy goodness with perfect crispy edges.

"Ok. If you say so." she says as she joins me with her cup of coffee and bowl of fruit.

"What's Malia up to this weekend? Maybe we can all check out the new Taraji movie." she asks, not knowing what she's unleashed.

"I don't know what she's up to, nor do I care." I say, stuffing way too much into my mouth.

My mom's eyes get wide, and then she squints, not knowing whether to broach the subject any further. But don't worry, she doesn't have to.

"Lia is probably off somewhere with her new little friend that she likes better because they have 'things in common' that she and I don't, so she needs to explore outside of our little bubble of friendship that we have had for almost 16 years!" I say, trying not to let the tears fall.

"Ahhhh. I see." my mom replies.

"And here I am all alone, looking like the fool with nothing to do because I haven't spoken to her most of the week and made our usual weekend plans since she actually has a weekend off from basketball." I continue.

"Mhmmm...so why don't you just text her?" Mom says as she grabs my plate to refill it.

"Seriously? What would I look like texting her? She needs to text me. She's the one who wants new friends." I say, slamming my glass of OJ in front of me.

"Well, you two will figure it out. Just my advice, though. Don't let it fester too long because it will become deep, and feelings will be hurt further, and then both of you will be sitting around looking like fools for no reason other than your own stubbornness." My mom says as she sets my plate down and turns up the music.

"The great Tina Turner sang 'What's love got to do with it' because she was hurt, but then she found love again because she put that stubborn attitude behind her," she said and started singing and bobbing her shoulders to the infamous song.

I stab at the pancakes and feel my phone buzz.

"Hey..." a text message from Malia says.

"Hey..." I responded back.

Mom, Tina, and the pancakes for the win.

Chapter 69

Holiday Classic Week

For anyone into sports holidays, Classics are the funnest weekends of the year in high school or college. Everyone at Ruth's Bader Ginsburg gets excited the week before the Classic. One, because it's the week before Winter Break, and two because we always play Sidwell in the championship games.

This year, we've decided to change our spirit week to this week so we go out with a bang. Today is school pride day, so I'm rocking my hair in two big afro-puffs, wearing an RBG t-shirt with a gavel in her hand that says "You down with RBG. Yeah, you know me," a pair of red cut-off shorts, knee high socks with blue stripes and a pair of red, white and blue high-top Chuck Taylors with red, white bottoms.

"Hey, Ari." I hear from behind me.

"Hey, Cai." I say, surprised. She's Nike'd down to the socks, all in school colors, with a shirt with RBG planking.

"Haven't seen you in a hot minute." I say, admiring her red Air Force 1s.

"Yeah, I've been really busy with indoor track, and I have tutoring during the week, so I haven't been able to hang much." she says, sounding some sort of way, but I just can't put my finger on it.

"Um, have you seen Lia?" she asks.

"Uh, not since the bus this morning." I say, trying not to sound suspicious.

"Oh, ok. She's not really responding to my text." she says, looking me square in the eye, trying to pull out information I don't have.

"Oh well, I'm sure she's just busy being Miss Popular," I say, trying to end the conversation.

"True..." she says with an awkward smile. "Well, if you do see her, tell her I'm looking for her." she says as she waves bye.

"Lawddd, what is going on now?" I say to myself, they just got back together at the Winter Social, "Hey you." Tyler says as he walks toward me, looking like someone straight out of a Vineyard Vines ad. Hair perfectly coiffed like his father, a bright smile, a pair of joggers and an RBG t-shirt that neatly reads "I DISSENT" in red and a pair of blue air maxes with red soles.

"Hey." I say, beaming a little too much.

"You look like the epitome of school spirit." he says to me with a little chuckle.

"Well, somebody has to represent." I say, putting my hands on my hips.

"Facts..." he says. "So, you wanna go grab something before the games start tomorrow?" He asks, his cheeks just the slightest pink.

"Sure, why not." I say. Russell is on the boys' team, so it's not like I had any other plans.

"Cool. I'll meet you at the center around 1." he says as he walks off with a little extra swag in his step.

"Ok." I say as I turn around and see Derrick and Erica walking up.

"Hey D., You ready for the weekend?" I ask. Derrick is the starting shooting guard for the team, and let me tell you, homeboy can shoot. I'm talking about Steph Curry shots. It also helps that he knows his power forward can rebound anything he doesn't make. Oh, did I mention Russell is the starting power forward? He can mix it up and play multiple positions, but nobody has his hops and strength like he does.

"Yup. Ready as I'll ever be." he says in that charming Southern accent.

"Hey, E!" I say as we hug and exchange air kisses.

"Hey, girl." she says. "I'm so happy I finally get to hang out on a weekend. Between dance class and working in a restaurant, I feel like I'm never around."

"Me too. I've missed you!" I say, putting my arm through hers as we walk down the hall. "So, we are all definitely hanging for at least a burger and milkshake after the games, right?" I say.

"Yes, ma'am." Derrick says as he spies Tyler and Russell and parts ways with us.

"So, what's going on?" Erica asks.

"Not much. Getting ready for a break and my dad's exhibit. Hanging with Russell..." I answer.

"Are y'all official yet or what? Dang girl, it's been almost 2 months." she says, chiding me.

"No. You know things are complicated, and I don't know..." I say, waving her off. But in my gut, I knew. Well, I think I know.

"Anyway, I'll see you tomorrow. Tyler and I are going to lunch before the games. Too bad you'll be stuck at dance class." I say nonchalantly.

"Wait a minute..." she says, holding my arm tightly in hers. "You and Tyler are going to lunch? Just the two of you? She asks, her eyes getting bigger as she moves closer to me.

"Uh yeah. Everyone is busy, and girls gotta eat!" I say, shrugging her off.

"Mhmmm," she says. "A girl in the middle of two teen GQ models must be starving."

"Omg. Gurl, bye." I say as I walk off to my last class.

As I walk off, I think to myself. What in the world is she talking about? Yeah, Tyler and I have gotten closer because he needs a friend who understands him and isn't going to judge him or just think of him as a bro. I like having heated discussions with him about politics, and sometimes I confide in him about my family drama, but that's just being a friend. Right?

Anyway, I'm going to take my school spirit to class and not think about it. Can't a girl just enjoy her favorite week of the year?

Chapter 70

Space Jams

Space Jams is another black cult classic with our hero, Micheal Jordan. Well, it's feeling like a great day to watch two of my favorite people kill it on the hardwood. But first, I need to figure out what I'm wearing to the game.

"Alexa, please play my Get Hype Mix." I say and start dancing around to old 90s dance songs that still seem to make it on every sporting events playlist.

As I dance around in my sweats, throwing things onto my bed. I can feel eyes on me.

I turn around, and my dad is there laughing hysterically.

"Ugh. Daddy, have you heard of announcing yourself before you walk in." I say, feigning annoyance.

"Oh, my bad, baby girl." he says, holding back more laughter. "I just couldn't get any words out when I watched you try to do the running, man," he says while imitating me.

"Uh, what are you talking about? That was the running man." I say, defending myself.

"What version was that?" He says, again trying to recreate what he saw.

"Um, the only one I know" I say, throwing my hands up.

"Um, well, I don't know what they are teaching y'all down at good ole RBG, but that's not it" as he starts doing some weird steps I've never seen.

"Uh, what is that?" I say as I fall onto my bed, laughing.

"Girl, y'all don't know anything about this right here." he says as he makes some weird motion with his hands and arms.

"Daddy, please stop, and don't ever do that outside of this house," I say as I push him out the door.

I sit down in my bed, Google 90s fashions, and think I have the perfect outfit.

"Hey, Ari." Tyler says as I walk into Taco Loco.

"Hey." I say, fixing my jeans.

"Um, you look nice." he says.

"Ha, thanks. I had a little 90s inspiration this morning, so I thought, go big or go home." I say as I sit down in my plaid skirt, tight RBG t-shirt with her wearing her dissent motif, my Doc Martens combat boots, and a pearl necklace I was able to make into a choker.

"Mhm" he says as he looks at the menu.

"So, isn't it nice to have basketball season off?" I say to start a conversation.

Tyler doesn't play basketball; actually, for being such an elite athlete, he's just plain awful at it. But he knows he's awful, so he doesn't even try to pretend like he's interested in playing even though he's the biggest Duke basketball fan I know and could tell you everything about the game. I guess he couldn't be great at everything.

"Yep. It gives me time to actually watch it." he says as he dips his chip into the salsa.

"It's my favorite time of the year too. Christmas and Kwanzaa are around the corner, then the new year!" I say, feeling giddy and hoping my parents have been getting the hint about Beyoncé or Doja Cat tickets.

"Yeah, I guess. My dad gets invited to more and more events, and my mom seems bored and lonely but still walks around with a smile on her face. I feel bad because I don't really want to go to them, so I make up excuses." He says, looking sadder than he should be during this time of the year.

"Well, whenever you want to watch that basketball game, let me know, and I'll come over, and I'll even bring the popcorn and Skittles." I say, trying to make him smile.

"You sure Russell won't care?" He asks, looking up at me.

"Why would he? He's so busy with basketball, and we are all just friends, so no, I don't think he would care, and he has no reason to." I say, sounding a little too on edge.

"Ok...whatever you say. Ready to order." he says as he waves for the server.

"Yeah, I'm starving." I say as I think about what Erica said yesterday.

Chapter 71

Game 6

"Give me a D…"

"Give me an I…" as the cheerleaders spell out our moniker and our mascot runs around in full RBG gear.

"What does that spell?"

"DISSENTERS!" we all yell as the mascot pounds her gavel to start the 2nd half.

Malia is killing it out there. She can play any position on the floor, and today, like always, she's our high scorer. She shot a buzzer-beater from half-court to end the 1st half, and everyone in the stands went crazy. You should have seen Mrs. and Mr. Wu cheer her on. Something is a little weird about it because they haven't been sitting next to each other at games, but you know how athletes and their families get about superstitions. So, I'm just going to ignore the weird feeling and keep cheering.

Russell walks up and sits next to us. "Hey, I have a few minutes before I have to go back in. You want to go grab a drink with me." he says, looking all shy.

"Sure." I say, knowing it's code for sneak a good luck kiss.

"So, what have you been up to all day?" He asks as we walk past the snack table.

"Not much. Went to lunch with Tyler and came here." I say, not thinking anything of it.

"Oh, I didn't know you guys were going to lunch," he says, trying not to sound surprised.

"Uh yeah. I thought I mentioned it. Anyway, we went to Taco Loco, and that was it," I say, feeling like I need to end the convo.

"Uh, ok. Cool," he says as he grabs my hand, pulls me toward him, and puts his forehead on mine.

"Hey," he smiles. "I really like you and your kisses," he says as he kisses the tip of my nose.

"Oh, do you?" I say, giggling.

"Yeah. I do," he says as he kisses my lips, and I kiss back.

Man, do I love his kisses?

"Well, I like you and your kisses, too," I say, pushing him away because it got hot in this corner. "Now get your butt back in the locker room and focus. I'll see you after the game number 33."

"Ok. Bet." he says as we walk back toward the gym, chatting about how he likes my outfit but how maybe I should stick to this decade. Ha, he has jokes.

Final: Girls: RBG 78 SWF 76 won by two free throws by Malia.

Boys: RBG 64 SWF 63 won on a buzzer-beater by Derrick.

MJ Game 6 buzzer beaters and good luck kisses are the best things about basketball.

"We Are...RBG".

Chapter 72

The Black Advent Calendar

You ask why we need a Black advent calendar. I don't know, but my mom is a Black history professor, and my dad is a renowned African-American artist, so my mom decided we should have a Black advent calendar. It's supposed to be something that is relevant to black culture, that's fun and educational. Oh, did I mention she makes the entire group do it?

Today's activity is Truth and Forgiveness. This activity entails telling someone that you love a truth or thought you have been holding on to, and the person has to be open to accepting your truth/thought and be open to forgive or let it go.

I hate this one and try to make it funny and tell my mom stuff like I hide peas in my pocket or tell my dad that he has flintstone feet, or tell Malia that she can't dance, or Russell that he can't sing. You know, fun stuff. But this year just doesn't feel the same. So, I'm going to avoid it all day because today is also our pre-Christmas Eve get-together with the crew because we all go off with our families or host our own family dinners on Christmas.

This year, it's being held at my house, which I love because we love to celebrate Christmas, and we love when the Channings volunteer to cater it.

"Ari, please come help me finish wrapping these presents for your friends!" my mom yells up the stairs as I play make-up artist in my mirror.

"Just a minute, Ma. Be right down," I say as I try to get this eyelash to stick. I can't wait until this eyelash trend dies because putting them on is for the birds, especially since my parents refuse to pay for someone to put a "weave" on my eyes, as they like to put it… but my eyes are poppin'.

I run down and start helping my mom wrap. She loves every moment of wrapping except tying the bow, which I love. I love making perfect bows and spiraling ribbons. We both get to work while listening to our Christmas playlist, the classics, the soul and R&B, children's song, N'Sync Christmas, and I occasionally sneak in a ratchet one that my mom just shakes her head at and sings along to anyway.

"So, have you done your activity for the day?" She asks as we sing Mariah Carey.

"Um, no. Something doesn't feel right about today. So, I'm still not sure who I'm going to say anything to or what my thought is."

"Don't tell anyone, but I felt the same way too. So I'm just going to enjoy my coquito and wait until I feel it in my spirit." My mom says as she takes another sip of Mr. Manning's famous coquito.

Side note: My mom only drinks on holidays or special occasions, and when she starts talking about feeling something in her spirit, I know it's going to be an eventful night.

Anyway, I get a text from Russell saying they are doing last-minute shopping, but they will be over soon. At that very moment, Malia walks through the door without her parents, and she's crying.

"Um, Hey Lia." I say as I jump up and rush over to her.

"Hey." she says as she falls onto the couch.

"What's going on, sweetie." my mom says as she walks over to sit with her on the couch.

"Ummmmm…" she says shakily. "We were all getting dressed, and I went to go ask my dad something…" she sniffles. "And I hear my mom say something about having to tell me about the separation soon." she says as she falls into my mom's lap, crying uncontrollably.

"Okay, sweetie. We are so sorry you had to hear that. Come on now, let's get you up to Ari's room." she says as she takes Malia's arm and leads her up the stairs. I follow up in disbelief.

"Malia. I am so sorry." I say, giving her a hug and sitting her down. Beyoncé doesn't have the divorce music she needs to hear right now.

"I just don't know why they've been keeping it a secret." she says. "I feel so dumb now; mom coming in.

late and sleeping in the guest room because she says she doesn't want to bother my father since he has early trials to prepare for." she continues as she shakes her head in disbelief.

"You are not dumb. It's not your responsibility to know every nuance of your parent's relationship, and you're certainly not responsible for being aware of them pulling apart," I say, trying to reassure her. "You're a kid with a life and a lot of other ish going on." I say, rubbing her back.

"I know, but still. I have a lot of stuff going through my head. My truth today was going to be telling Cai I think we need a break because we never have time for each other, and I don't want it to ruin our friendship." she says, trying to wipe away her tears.

"Well, damn. You were going for the truth, truth today, huh?" I say, looking extra surprised.

"Um, okay, how about we hold onto that little piece of truth and get back to the here and now." I say, pacing back and forth. Thinking about how these eyelashes are going to waste because I'm about to cry them off. My poor friend.

"Ugh, I don't even want to deal with them." She says as she lays back on my bed, bringing her knees to her chest.

"I know. I know. But they didn't know you were there, and they at least get a chance to say their truth.

Remember, that's the point of the day. To let go and forgive if we can." I say, finally understanding why my mom does this stupid calendar. Sometimes, people just need a safe space. I feel so bad for the entire Wu family. They are my other family.

Right then, there's a knock on my door. "Hold on," I say. Walking over to it and cracking it. I see Mr. and Mrs. Wu standing there with bloodshot eyes.

"Um. Yeah, she's in here." I say, trying to figure out what to do.

They both walk in, both looking as distraught as Lia. "Ari, will you give us a moment." Mr. Wu says, his beautiful almond eyes red with tears.

"Yeah, sure, of course." I say as I back my way out of my room. Watching to see if Malia needs it. She nods her head at me, and I close the door and rip off the eyelashes.

"Hey, Ari." Russell says, standing at the bottom of the stairs with his hands in his black and grey sweatpants pockets, rocking back and forth on his heels.

"Ugh, Hey. Let's go outside real quick." I say as I grab his hand and walk out without saying anything to anyone. That is a big no in the black household, but baby Jesus, throw me a bone! I need air.

"What the hell is going on in there? The adults all went into the kitchen and told me to stay in the living room," Russell says, totally confused.

"What are you always worried about with your moms? But they seem to have the relationship of Beyoncé and Jay-Z." I say because I just can't stand saying the word divorce.

"Oh no! Seriously? I did not see that coming." Russell says as he massages his forehead.

"Apparently, neither did Lia. Because she is in complete shock and is pissed beyond belief." I say.

"Was that supposed to be their 'truth' today?" He asks.

"I dunno, but it is now." I say, exasperated.

"Okay. Well, we need to warn Erica and Eric before they walk into this storm." He says as he grabs his phone and starts texting like a madman.

We walk back inside, and everyone except Malia and her parents are sitting there, trying not to look awkward.

"Hi, Mrs. Audra. Hi, Mrs. Sara." I say with an awkward smile.

"Hey." they say in unison and take a sip of wine.

"The Channings will be over any minute," my mom says, jumping up. "Let's all look alive, people!" She starts ordering people around because that's her way of reducing stress, and we all fall in line and get busy.

Russell and I are setting the table when Malia comes down and starts helping. We all continue in silence until Erica gets there and in good ole island fashion.

"Malia. Omg. Come here." She walks in, arms wide open, ready to envelop Malia in one of her big hugs.

Malia obliges and lets Erica wrap her up and rock her while she cries. Russell and I walk out to get more stuff and sigh a breath of relief. Thank God for Erica. She is the mama bear of all of us.

The parents are chatting and doing their thing, trying to ignore the elephant in the room. But we all know it's going to be sitting in the middle of the table when we sit down to eat.

"Okay, everyone, let's gather around and say grace and then dig into this beautiful meal the Channings have made us." My dad says, trying to lighten the mood.

We all bow our heads for grace, and I feel Russell squeezing my hand and can't help but think how happy I am to have him here.

Miraculously, we make it through dinner without any obvious hiccups. The dads have dish duty, aka, so they can go out and smoke cigars while the kids and moms go and get the presents sorted. Mrs. Sara usually goes and hangs out with the dads, but she hates cigars, so she's more than happy to be with us.

"Hey, can I talk to you?" Russell says as the moms sing to Destiny Child's Christmas.

"Yeah, sure." I say as I follow him down the hall.

"Okay…" he clears his throat like he's going to give a speech.

"Okay…" I say, standing up straight, ready to listen, not knowing what's about to hit me.

"Ari. I really like you. You're my best friend, and like I said, I love your kisses, your smile lights up the room, you are so intelligent and super feisty and passionate, and I admire those things about you," he pauses.

"Well, thank you, Mr. Black-Summers. That's a great "truth."

"Is it my turn now?" I say, poking him in the shoulder.

"Um. No." he says.

"Ummm, okay. Continue, I guess."

"Thanks," he clears. "With all that being said. Ari… I–"

"Hey! Let's go, you two. Everyone's ready to open presents."

"Ugh. Okay." he says, frustrated. "Hold that thought." He looks at me as he turns and walks toward the living room.

Um, was he going to say he hates when I wear eyelashes? Or he hates it when I boss everyone around. Of course, I'm going to hold that thought because I have to be prepared to forgive or let go.

"Okay, y'all. Everyone, take a number, and we'll start White Elephant." my mom says.

The game was hilarious. I ended up with a Santa who twerks.

As everyone parted ways, I could see Malia did not want to go home.

"Hey, you want to stay here tonight?" I nudge her.

"Do you mind?" She says hopefully.

"Seriously?!" I say. "Go ask your parents, and I'll ask mine.

"Okay." she says as she walks toward her parents.

I see the parents make eye contact and nod that it's okay, and Malia comes running back, saying she'll be right back. She just needs to grab her head scarf.

Russell grabs me out of nowhere like a thief in the night and pulls me to a corner.

"Okay, let me make this quick even though it wasn't my plan, and please don't interrupt, and no, it's nothing bad." he says.

I stand there and don't say a peep.

"Ari, I like you, and I want to know if you will be my girlfriend. Like girlfriend-girlfriend. Like, tell people you're my girlfriend?"

"Uhhhhhhhh. Hold on a minute." I say, taking a deep breath. I was not expecting this.

"Russell, let's go, boy!" I hear Mrs. Audra call from around the corner.

"Coming, mama." he yells back.

"Can we discuss this tomorrow?" he says as he backs away.

"Uh yeah. Let's do that." I say, looking puzzled.

"Okay, cool." He comes back toward me and lays a kiss on me that would put fireworks to shame.

"Cool." is all I muster up and wave goodbye.

This Truth and Forgiveness Day has been too much for my little heart. I need some sparkling cider and Beyoncé to get me through this.

Chapter 73

Sade

"I just aspire to pick people up. That's my ambition."

- Sade Adu.

I wake up and stretch. Last night was an emotional night, Malia trying to deal with her parents' separation and the thing with Cai. On top of it all, I'm dealing with Russell asking me to be his girlfriend. I cherish his friendship so much, but like Sade always says, "Your love is the sweetest taboo." How do you balance those two things? Also, on a very selfish note, I don't think my parents got me those Beyoncé or Lizzo tickets. Your girl is feeling every emotion in the book.

I turn over and see a text from Tyler.

"Happy Christmas Eve. Miss ya!" It says.

Okay...when did we start saying miss ya to each other? Add confusion to my list of emotions.

"Malia," I whisper and nudge her. She breathes heavily and turns over.

"Malia. Girl, wake up!" I say as I shake her shoulder.

"Seriously, Ariana!" She says as she turns over and gives me a death stare.

"Yes. Read this." I say as I shove the phone into her face.

She barely opens her eyes to read it. "Okay, well, tell your boyfriend you miss him back. Did you really wake me up for this?" She says as she attempts to roll back over.

"First, Russell is not my boyfriend. And second, that doesn't even matter because the text is from Tyler!" I say, my voice is a little more panicked than I would like.

"Oh snap. Tyler is missing you?" She says as she jumps up and with big eyes.

I get up and start messing around with stuff on my desk. "I mean, it's not deep. We are friends now. You and I say we miss each other, right?" I say, trying to convince the both of us.

"Uh yeah, but we've been friends for our entire lives, and it's quite obvious that Tyler likes you." she says matter-of-factly.

"He does not like me. It's Tyler, for goodness' sake." I say not so convincingly.

"Okay. Sit down." Malia says as she sits up, head scarf half off. "Tyler likes you, girl. He is always hanging around us and has been sitting at our lunch table half of the time. Y'all go out for "friendly" ice cream dates when Russell is busy. He has asked you over to watch games, and the most obvious thing is the way he looks at you when you pass him in the hallway." she says, crossing her.

arms. "Russell isn't dumb! He gives Tyler the death-stare any time he stares too long, but he also knows you're clueless and in your own world half the time, so he doesn't show you that he's jealous because he's Russell, and he adores you and your aloof-ness," she says, looking like she's waiting for a light bulb to pop up over my head.

"I mean. I guess. You know. Ugh. I don't know what's going on here. I like Russell, you know, like him, like him. He makes me laugh and makes me feel all, ya know. I like Tyler; I like hanging out because he makes me laugh, and we have really good debates. But I don't want to be Tyler's girlfriend." I say, feeling super annoyed with myself.

"Well, you in danger, girl. You better figure out what you're going to do with your boos before it's too late." she says as she heads toward the bathroom.

"Uh, me. You gotta figure your life out with Cai." I say defensively as she slams the door shut.

Dammit, why can't a girl have an ordinary love and not this sweet taboo triangle that's developed right in front of me?

Chapter 74

India Arie

*"To spread love, healing, peace, and joy is my mission in life
— and so I speak up."*

- India Arie.

Have you ever listened to India Arie? So sweet and melodic. Beautiful love songs about Black love. Well, you should. Because she perfectly sums up my parents.

I walk into the kitchen and see my dad and mom wrapped tight around each other, swaying to India Arie, my mom's chin on his chest, and my dad placing tiny kisses on her forehead. Listen, their marriage isn't always peaches and cream. They argue, they sometimes go days without talking, and my dad even gets put on the couch, but every time, they come back together stronger than ever. Love ebbs and flows with life. I get that because I watch them. I see the flirting, the tiny kisses, and the adoring eyes. I see the deep talks they have with one another about life, spirituality, art, and education. I see and feel how they love me every day unconditionally. That's the kind of love I want one day.

"Morning. Ew, can y'all please get a room." I say as I grab water from the fridge.

"Um, little girl, we pay the bills, so every room is ours," my mom says as she turns around to pour herself another cup of coffee.

"So, what do we want to do before the grandparents get here tonight?" My dad asks.

It's our little family tradition to do something fun on Christmas Eve. Last year, we went ice skating, and I almost broke my leg. The year before that, we did an indoor ropes course, and dad wouldn't jump at the end because he's afraid of heights.

"How about we do something that doesn't require physical activity," my mom says. "Especially since y'all are lacking the athletic gene." she snickers as she sips her coffee.

"Whatever!" I say, acting offended.

"Listen, being scared of heights has nothing to do with athletic ability." my dad says, trying to stand up tall and show off his muscles.

"Well, I was thinking we would do something more generous. So, I volunteered us to help feed the homeless," she says, looking quite proud of herself.

"Cool. I'm down for that." I say. As long as I can wear sweatpants and not have to sweat, I'm good.

"Great. The Mannings are hosting the event, so we have to look somewhat put together." she says as she gets up and pushes in her chair.

"What?" I shriek and then try to clear my throat. "I mean, what? I can't wear sweats?"

"Nope. Jeans will do, and no over-the-top t-shirts. I'm sure the media will be there," she says as she walks off and sneaks a little pat on my dad's backside.

He follows with a big smile.

"Why is this happening to me?" I say as I walk up the stairs, trying to figure out what I'm going to do and figure out what an over-the-top t-shirt means.

"Mayday! Mayday!" I text Malia.

"What's up, girl?" She replies.

"My mom volunteered us to help feed the homeless with the Mannings."

"Wide-eyed emoji, laughing emoji, monkeys covering their mouths, eyes, and ears emoji," she replies.

"Mouth wide open emoji, mind-blown emoji, girl running emoji," I reply back.

"Well, I guess you can tell Tyler face to face that you miss him too, LOL emoji," she replies.

"Girl, bye. Oh, tell Cai hey for me, side-eye emoji" I reply.

"Mad emoji, eye-roll emoji" she replies.

"Kiss emoji." I end the convo.

This is going to be an interesting day. I think I'll either wear my "I am Not My Hair" or my "Brown Skin" T-shirt.

What? They don't seem over the top to me.

Chapter 75

Not Today, Devil...

I walk into the facility and immediately spot Tyler in his khakis and a buttoned-up polo shirt with rolled-up sleeves. The epitome of a politician's kid. His dad and mom basically have on the same exact thing. My mom thought my shirt was too political, so we compromised on a t-shirt with MLK, Jr. wearing a Santa hat. What? It's festive.

"Hey there." Tyler says as he walks over.

"Hi, Mr. and Mrs. Whitaker. Thank you for coming." he says as he shakes their hands.

"Hi. Tyler. We are very pleased to be here," my mom replies. "I'm going to go over and say hi to your parents. She says as she grabs my dad's hand and leaves us standing there alone. Awkward!

"Hey." I say, looking down on the floor.

"Hey." he says, doing the same.

"Happy Christmas Eve." I say, minus the miss ya part.

"Yeah, Happy Christmas Eve." he says, smiling. Boy, that smile will get ya every time.

"So please stand next to me so we can get through this together." he says as he leads me toward the serving area.

"You're so funny." I say. "This is for a great cause."

"I know, but everything is so political these days, and the media is here, and I just want someone to talk to. Luckily for me, it's you." he says as he looks back over his shoulder, his Mediterranean blue eyes smiling at me.

Mayday! Mayday! Ariana! Abort! Abort! Do not look into his eyes.

"Uh yeah. It is lucky for you that my sparkling personality is gracing this event." I say, trying to sound sarcastic.

As we walk up to the area to begin serving, I get a text from Russell.

"Hey, you. Happy Christmas Eve! Hope you're having a good day. Pink heart emoji, black heart emoji."

Everything in me shifts, and I'm smiling for no reason.

"Pink heart emoji. Christmas tree emoji. Santa emoji.

Black heart emoji." I reply back.

The afternoon goes by quickly, and I hug Tyler and his parents goodbye and thank them for hosting such a wonderful event.

"That was a lot of fun." I say as we get into the car.

"Yeah, it was." my mom says as she looks at me through the rearview mirror. "So, Tyler has a little crush, I see." she says.

"Uh, no. That's my boy. We just have a good time together."

"Mhmmm." she replies as my dad gets into the car.

"OK, who's ready to go skydiving?" My mom says as she looks at my dad, who gives her the biggest stank eye and starts the car.

"Not today, devil." I say, laughing hysterically.

Chapter 76

Christmas Day

I wake up, and I smell food! All the food, especially that bacon my mom is cooking for Christmas breakfast.

"Good morning!" I say as I come running down the stairs. I know I'm 15 and I know there's no Santa but tell me how all these presents got put under the tree when my parents went to bed at the same time as me? That's what I thought.

I can hear music playing as I hit the last step. Silent Night by the Temptations. Would it even be Christmas without hearing this multiple times a day between Thanksgiving and the Lord's birthday?

"Good morning, Ari." Grand Daddy says to me as he puts his walking shoes on and sings along to the music. The man walks 4 miles a day without fail.

"Good morning, Boo Thang!" My dad calls out from his office. His show is in two days, so he has been working non-stop.

"Good morning, bumble bee." my Mama G says as she's washing her greens for the 5th time, I bet. She calls me Bumble Bee because she says I'm always buzzing around in everybody's business. I have no clue what she's talking about…

"Morning, Mommy," I say as I kiss her on the cheek and steal a piece of bacon before she can smack my hand.

"Morning, Lovebug." she says as she booty bumps me out of her way.

I send a group text out to the crew: "Wakey, wakey. Eggs and bakey! It's Christmas Day, y'all! Miss you all and hope you get everything you want and pray these people I call parents got me my concert tickets."

"Merry Christmas! I got the new iPhone!!!" Erica replies.

"Merry Christmas! I got the limited-edition Jordans," Malia replies.

"Hey! Hey! Merry Christmas." Russell replies.

And then a picture of a BMW pops up, sunglasses emoji, car emoji, melted face emoji."

"Damnnnnnn flame emoji, mad emoji, tongue-out emoji," I reply.

We all LOL and say our goodbyes.

I don't turn 16 until the summer, so there won't be a Lexus with a red bow sitting in my driveway. Nor will there be one in the summer.

"OK, let's open gifts." I yell out to everyone.

We all gather around the tree and parse out gifts. My mom puts on some classical Christmas music, and basically, everyone sits back because my pile of gifts is exponentially bigger than anyone else's.

As I unwrap my gifts, I say thank you and give out hugs and kisses. I laugh when I open a new American Girl doll because grandma Whitaker thinks I still collect them, but I hold it tight, give her a kiss, and thank her.

As everyone gets up to go back to cooking, I start to head up to my room to put stuff away.

"Hey." my mom calls out as I hit the first step.

"Hey…" I say, craning my neck, trying not to drop stuff. I hate making multiple trips.

"You want some help with that stuff." she says as she comes up behind me.

"Nah, I'm good." I say as I start making my way up.

"OK." she says as she follows me up.

"What are you doing, Mom?" I ask as I struggle to get to the last step.

"Nothing, just coming up here to see all the stuff you got." she says.

"Oh. Weren't you just down there? I'm so confused." I say as I turn around and see her smiling with an envelope in her hand.

"Ummmmm, what is that? I ask, trying not to get too excited because it could just be an envelope with nothing in it.

"I don't know, open it and see." she says with a devilish smile.

I grab the envelope quickly because I don't want whatever's in it to disappear, and 4 tickets slip out. Two to Beyoncé and two to Doja Cat.

"Oh, my gawd." I scream. "Omg, omg, omg!" I say out loud! "Thank you so much, mommy!" I hug her so tight I feel like I might break her!

I run down the stairs to my dad's office. "Omg, Daddy! Thank you so much." I whisper because he's on a phone call.

He smiles super big and does the cabbage patch, and I roll my eyes because he's such a nerd.

I immediately grab my phone and text the crew a picture of me smiling with the tickets: "heart eye emoji, parent and child emoji, 3 red heart emojis."

"Niceeeee." Russell texts back.

"I got dibs on, Doja." Malia texts back.

"I'm just fine with the Beyoncé ones." Erica texts back.

"I'll drive ya!" Russell texts back.

All in All, today was a good day (in my Ice Cube voice)!

Is it time to eat dinner yet?

Chapter 77

Jean-Michel Basquiat

"I'm not a real person. I'm a legend."

- Jean-Michel Basquiat.

Today is the day. Dad's big art exhibition. He has declined all media for the opening so that his closest family and friends will be the first to see pieces that have been exhibited overseas and the new pieces he is debuting. I'm so excited for him that I can hardly contain myself.

Today is also the day Malia and I have chosen to tell everyone how we feel.

"So, I told Cai to meet me at Taco Loco for lunch," Malia texts me.

"OK. How are you doing?" I ask.

"I'm freaking out a little bit. I think it's for the best," she says.

"OK, text me after." I reply.

"OK, and I'll see you tonight." she replies.

"Cool. Stay strong, bestie." I reply and put my phone down, roll back over, and go to sleep.

It's much easier for me to deal with her business than my own. So, I just won't until I need to tonight.

"Ari! Come down so we can have our make-up done my mom says after she hears me step out of the shower.

"OK. I'll be right down." I say.

Even though it's a no-media night, it's still a formal event in a prestigious venue, so we have to get all fancy.

"I'm so excited for your father." my mom says, looking as beautiful as ever. Ruby red lips against her cinnamon skin.

"Me too. I'm happy he gets to be home for a while."

I say.

"Me too."

"Don't go making any more babies you can't afford." I say jokingly, but I'm serious.

"Girl, bye. I'm trying to get my retirement fund in order and you out of my house." she says.

"What do you mean out of the house? I thought you wanted me to live here forever." I say, acting sad and offended.

"No, ma'am. You cost too much, and me and your daddy need some privacy." she says, trying to look serious but can't hide the smile.

"Privacy? Y'all don't need any privacy. Y'all aren't grown," I say, trying to stay still as Erica's aunt puts on the finishing touches. Guess what? I got to get eyelash extensions, aka eye weave, for this event. Yasssss! Erica's aunt for the win!

Chapter 78

Black and Red Carpet

As we walk down the black and red carpet, I look at my parents. My mom, in a beautiful red gown, represents her sorority to the fullest. Her hair is pulled into a beautiful golden bun with her edges laid and her face beat to the gawds and my dad admiring her, lookin' like Denzel circa 2002, his black suit and red bow tie to compliment my mom. I decided on a gown to compliment them both, a black and red ombre sequined dress with red heels and my hair in perfect twist out. I'm so proud to be a part of the Whitaker crew.

"Wow!" Russell says as he stares at me as I walk through the entrance.

"Um, boy, stop staring." I say as I hit him in the shoulder.

"Well, I'm just sayin'." he keeps staring.

"Let's go get something to drink and find the others." I say.

"Heyyyyy!" I yell to everyone over the music. "Hey!" Malia and Cai say at the same time. "Um, hey..." I say, confused.

"It's all good, Ari. We both thought it was for the best." Cai says as she looks at Malia.

"Oh, that's great." I say as I wrap them up in a big hug.

"Heyyyyyy, gorgeous! Are those lash extensions?"

Erica says as she pulls Derrick behind her. Her parents really like Derrick, so they let him hang around as long as Eric is around.

"What's good?" Tyler says as he walks up and fist bumps his bros.

"Heyyy, Ari..." he says as he gives me the up down.

"Hey." I say, feeling like something is on my face.

"Well, let's dance before we eat." Erica says, ending the awkward moment and leading us all to the dance floor.

After dinner, we have the best time, and I'm going around dancing with everyone; my mom and dad are doing the wobble and the Cupid shuffle, and then the DJ puts on a slow song, and everyone finds their partner. I see my dad grab my mom, and even the Wus are dancing. Of course, Russell literally just left to go to the bathroom, and so here I am standing partner-less.

"May I have this dance?" I hear Tyler say as he walks up from behind me.

"Sure. Why not?" I say, putting my hands on his shoulders and swaying awkwardly to the music.

"So, Ari. I just wanted to tell you how much I appreciate you for being here for me this year. It's been so cool getting to know you again." he says while trying not to step on my feet.

"Well, thank you, Tyler. I feel the same way. Even though you're still a Bernie bro, I like having you around too." I say with a big smile.

"Well, there's something else I want to tell you." He clears his throat.

"Um, OK..." I respond.

"Well, I know it's obvious, and I've been trying to talk myself out of it, but I like you a lot. Now, I know you and Russell have a thing, and I'm not going to step on my boys' toes, but I like you, and I need you to know that. But I also want you to know that I like having our friendship. So, I'm putting it out there so it's off my chest and not so awkward, and I respect you and Russell and your space." he says, finally taking a breath.

"Um..." I smile awkwardly. "Look, Tyler. I think you're awesome, and you're cute."

"Oh yeah. You think I'm cute?" He interrupts me, giving me that smile. Dreamy, I tell ya.

"Yes, you're cute, little baby GQ with perfectly coiffed hair, striking eyes, a bright white smile, and an extensive vocabulary most days," I say. "Everyone knows you're cute or whatever." I continue. "Anyway, I like having you as a friend I can talk to about stuff my other.

friends don't want to talk about, and I don't want to jeopardize that." I say, taking another deep breath. "And I like Russell, and I think he's my boyfriend." I say, sounding almost confident.

"Oh yeah? Am I?" Russell says as he walks up, smiling.

"Hey, bro, do you mind if I cut in?" He says to his friend.

"Of course, dude." Tyler says. "Take care of her." he whispers into Russell's ear and squeezes my arm.

Russell nods and takes my hand. "So, when were you going to tell me I was your boyfriend?" he says, giving me his infamous side smile.

"Where did you hear that?" I say, smiling slyly.

"Oh, I heard a rumor. But it's not Facebook official, so I didn't believe it." he says, putting his hands on my waist.

"Well, we should do something about that, huh?" I say as I pull out my phone and snap a picture of me kissing my boo...on the cheek (I don't want my mama whooping me) with his big Kool-Aid smile taking up the entire pic and posting it on Facebook, Instagram and Snapchat.

"Heart eyes emoji, boyfriend/girlfriend emoji, queen emoji, king emoji, pink heart emoji, black heart emoji.".

I look at him. "I guess that makes it official. I'll let you be MY boyfriend." I say, laughing.

"Okayyyy. Thank you for the honor of being YOUR boyfriend." He laughs, pulls me in tighter, and kisses my forehead.

I rest my head on his chest and smile.

I think it's going to be a happy new year for the crew! Cheers!

The End.